GO HARD OR GO HOME

WHO IS SHYDOW?

D1240576

RUSSELL L MABRY

Book and Cover design by AuthorPackages
First Edition: 2013

ISBN: 978-1947732797

ACKNOWLEDGMENTS

First and foremost, I would like to acknowledge GOD in the name of Jesus Christ, for with him all things are possible.

I would like to give a special thanks to Wahida Clark for her help in bringing my vision to life!

Dedicated to any and everyone in the struggle. Understand that you can overcome everything.

CHAPTER 1

III

"BACK 2 DA FUTURE"

I t was the darkest of nights in the life of Norcotic. The type
of murkiness that could engulf a closed casket making death
afraid of the absence of light. The type of dark that could
make silence seem loud. In the midst of this deafening quiet,
dressed to match such ear- piercing placidity, Norcotic wiped
perspiration from his hands ensuring that his Teflon
bulletproof vest and weapons of war stayed secured. The
weight of the equipment was similar to the weight upon his
shoulders. What was even heavier on the heart was the fact that
only violence of the most gruesome nature could remove the
burden. After ridding his hands of nervous sweat along his
black tactical gear, Norcotic applied latex, then leather gloves
on his hands. Lastly, he concealed his identity with a black ski
mask.

Besides the company of four that tagged along to assist
with the mission, Norcotic's only protection was the two twin
Desert Eagles strapped to his gun holster, which he now pulled
for motivation. The mission: Get the MONEY! And that

alone, besides loyalty, was the only reason for the five-man team being assembled, camouflaged with the dark of the night, and prepared for an attack. Crouched low in the wooded surroundings that blocked the present target from observing them, the team of men were putting a conclusion to their surveillance. Reloading every bullet in the Desert Eagle, Norcotic thought about the past events, and how they led to the present moment. With each bullet applied to the clips, the memories flooded Norcotic's brain in a way that Noah's Ark would have been submerged in an ocean…

Block was exercising in his prison cell, which was comical in a sense because he was so big; he made the tiny space seem smaller than what it was. Block was 15 years into a murder bid and working out was the only way to relieve his tension. Every day he thought about the decisions and bullets that killed his victims and affected his son's life. There was a possibility of freedom even though he was sentenced to life in prison, but in order to receive autonomy, he needed his son, Norcotic, to live a life he never intended for him to experience. Freedom came with a price that the poorest people could not afford. But as broke as Block was emotionally, he was willing to pay with his soul and sacrifice his family as if he was applying for a position within the Illuminati.

Norcotic was due to visit Block at the maximum-security prison facility that housed Block along with the world's most dangerous humans turned animals. As Block did his 2000 reps of pushups, he was not surprised to hear the guard yell his name. "Russell Leroy Gray! You have a visit." Block stood up slowly and calmed himself to see his son.

Norcotic sat behind the bulletproof glass that separated the visitors from the prisoners. Just to have access to the medieval looking structure was a yearlong process. One had to get clearance from the FBI and a recommendation from the visitor's state governor, which in Norcotic's case was Douglas Wilber of Virginia. That was easily done because Governor Wilber was involved in Block's case. Norcotic received a message over a year ago to start the process that had him sitting inside of hell meeting the devil himself.

The message explained there was a way for Block to receive freedom. Being denied a father in his life due to Block's incarceration, made Norcotic willing to do whatever was needed to have his father released from prison. Sitting on the backless, metal stool, Norcotic watched Satan himself stroll into the visitation room. He wondered why his dad had to be chained and shackled along with an armed guard as an escort when there was bulletproof glass, three inches thick that separated the two of them. Norcotic looked up at his father whom he had not seen since the age of three and thought, What the Fuck! This nigga is huge! Block was 5'10 and weighed a staggering 260 pounds of muscle that bulged from his prison jumper threatening to escape, as if reflecting Block's thought of escaping prison. Block looked at his son and thought, Shit! This little motherfucker isn't ready for war, looks like I'm stuck in this hellhole. The two men stared at each other and saw two very different people, but both had the same exact feelings of anger and love.

"You have 10 minutes!" The guard informed them.

"Damn! A year of waiting, and 12 hours of driving just for ten minutes!" Norcotic voiced and received a stern expression from the guard. Norcotic and Block sat down as the prison

3

guard left them alone, giving Block the privacy he needed to transfer the coded message. That message had Norcotic and his team sitting outside the three-story mansion that housed the target, and the keys to unlock the door to Block's freedom…

Coming back to the present, but still mentally in the past, Norcotic thought, *After all these years of not seeing me, his only son, all that mattered was this mission. He didn't even say that he loves me.* As Norcotic thought about his fatherless life, Ice snapped him out of his daydream and back to reality.

"Norcotic! Norcotic! Mane, Norcotic! Snap back, nigga. What the fuck is wrong with you?"

"Nothing nigga, I'm focused," Norcotic replied to a concerned Ice.

"Yeah, aight nigga, you better be because we can't afford to be fucking this shit up. I'm too pretty to go to prison, nigga; you feel me, Nor?"

"Yeah I hear you, shawdy," Norcotic replied in his Richmond, Virginia slang to Ice's New Jersey slur.

Being clear that the mission was underway, things started to feel like the movie *Menace II Society* when Caine and O-Dog were arguing before whacking the niggas that killed Caine's cousin Harold at the traffic light. As if life was playing a part of the moment, Ice further elaborated.

"For real, Norcotic, don't be acting like no bitch when shit gets poppin'!"

"Mane shut the fuck up, Ice!" Norcotic harshly whispered while placing both Desert Eagles back in their respective holsters.

"Yo, both of y'all niggas need to chill before we get caught out back in this bitch," Killa said while eyeing his surroundings, making sure no one was embarking upon their hideout.

Sincere also added his discomfort. "I definitely agree. They have guard dogs all throughout the compound, plus the estate is built with material in such a way that faraway sounds echo. It was part of the development given as a precaution for extra security."

Sincere was in charge of scoping out the mansion before the mission, and frankly, it was obvious the man had done his job.

"Son, I'm just trying to get this money, and get the fuck out of here!" E-Youngin impatiently said while anxiously tapping his foot, aggravated by his team's stalking low approach to completing the task.

"We gon make the move when the time is right! Everybody tighten the fuck up!" Norcotic said with his eyes bugged out of his head as if his eyes were about to explode. This gave his men the reminder that Norcotic had an uncontrollable temper evident by the dynamite in his pupils. The five-man team were members of the organization M.A.F.A.R. MAFIA that was eight members deep. The other three members, Tiny, Mouse, and Ice's brother, Legion, were waiting back at their headquarters for their arrival and the completion of the robbery.

Ice and Norcotic started M.A.F.A.R. MAFIA. The two met when Norcotic was in the second grade; Ice had moved to Richmond, Virginia from Newark, New Jersey. Even though he was two years older than Norcotic and in the fourth grade, the two became fast friends because Norcotic came to Ice's aid when he was being jumped by people in the neighborhood. They were not kind to people from out of town. Ever since that day, the two were thick as thieves.

M.A.F.A.R. began focusing on the Governor's Mansion

whose occupants were government officials, Governor Wilber and his wife, Judge Snuckles-Wilber, who was the Honorable that sentenced Norcotic's father, Block, to life in prison for murder.

Block was a ruthless killer from the Blackwell community of Southside Richmond, convicted of a murder he did not commit. At the time, it was 1989, and Norcotic was only three years old, so Block did everything he could to receive a pardon for his innocence. The rumor was that Block's brother was the triggerman, but not wanting to see his brother in a situation that would devastate his mother, Block took the murder rap. For the lack of DNA and no witnesses, Block was released and compensated $500,000 in a verdict that proved his innocence. Back on the streets again, Block killed a well-known drug boss named Clayton Brown.

Clayton Brown was second in charge of the vicious gang known by Brown Brothers Gang. Block was a well-respected hit man, and by killing Clayton Brown on the day he was pardoned from a murder charge, everybody knew there was more to the killing than just a hit; Block was making a statement. What would have been more shocking is if they knew that Governor Wilber had hired Block to assassinate Clayton Brown. Governor Wilber was using the Richmond City Police to blackmail drug dealers in Richmond City. He took their kilos of cocaine and resold them at a higher price to New York City clientele who were seeking the cheaper prices that southern states had to offer. Clayton Brown was not your average hustler, he was a very smart man. Being the main target of the governor's harassment, he always took pictures and recorded videos of their business transactions.

The pictures and videos were recorded without Douglas

Wilber's knowledge, but almost every hustler from Virginia knew because Clayton Brown would boast about his plan to dethrone Douglas Wilber from the governor's seat. Block knew of this information, and while he was incarcerated for a murder he never committed, he informed Douglas Wilber of the incriminating evidence that would land him in prison for years. The threat of those pictures and videos being released to the Press prompted Douglas Wilber to make a hell of a deal with Lucifer. Those same pictures and videos caused the death of Clayton Brown and made Block a legend within the history of Richmond, Virginia.

Block was hired for $500, 000—the amount rewarded to him for his wrongful conviction—to kill Clayton Brown and retrieve the evidence that could destroy the governor. After the mission was complete, Block was surprised to find out that when delivering the pictures and videos, instead of his compensation, he was given steel handcuffs to accommodate his arrest for murder. Block was set-up. The governor never paid Block the money he hoped to use to give his son, Norcotic, a better life, nor did he try to use his title as governor to help with the case. Actually, it was promoted as just another black man being a savage to the community due to the fact that the governor pardoned him for murder only for him to be released and do what he was pardoned for.

The Press reported the death of Clayton Brown as retaliation for the murder of Lil Lesley, who was killed by Rahkee, a hit man hired by the kingpin Eugene Johnson, who was an associate of the Brown Brothers Gang. Lil Lesley was Block's best friend, but Block summed his death up to the street life and charged it to the game. The hit was never retaliation. Only one other person knew the truth and that was the single parent that raised Norcotic. Now, sixteen years later, Norcotic sat with M.A.F.A.R. outside of the Governor's Mansion. $500,000, the pictures, and videos were the mission at hand, and securing the kitty seemed nearly impossible from the security set up around the mansion.

Irritated from the defenses protecting the entrance to the mansion, Norcotic spoke to his team, "Who was in charge of layout?"

Norcotic had been watching the habits of the governor's security through a miniature high-powered telescope and did not like what he had seen. The reply came from the baby faced Sincere who looked much like the rapper Memphis Bleek, and truly deserved the resemblance because right now Norcotic wanted to *roc* him like Jay- Z.

"Every time I did my round, there was never this much security on the premises," Sincere spoke, confused, while scratching his temple with the barrel of his semi-automatic.

"I don't give a fuck how many niggas in that bitch; I'm ready to get paid!" Ice added, rubbing his shotgun like the head of the Mob rubs his pet cat.

"I don't know," Killa's opinion interrupted the exchange, "Norcotic's right! There are a total of ten guys on the post."

M.A.F.A.R. was not prepared for the extra security, but Norcotic was motivated to complete the task. Nodding his head to what Killa said, E-Youngin was now thinking they should abort the mission.

Norcotic ignored all of the vibes from his crew. While he was second in command, he was the one who was leading the current event. He took control with the swagger of a leader.

"Look! One man is walking around the Mansion clockwise while his partner is doing the same but counterclockwise. This way, they both cover each other's post when they aren't present and it gives them both a meeting spot to cross paths, alerting one another of any danger. There are also four men by the gate, and four more by the front door. We are clueless to how many guards may be inside and to what is in the back of the Mansion, but it has to be protected due to how many men are protecting the front. This is the plan, Killa, when I give the signal over the walkie-talkie, which would be me screaming Go, throw a grenade at the front gate, then get inside, find the judge, and create a hostage situation. Once that's done, Ice and only Ice will meet me in the master bedroom." Norcotic waited for any objections from his team, after receiving not one rebuttal, he asked, "Is everybody clear?"

The only response was the sound of various weapons being activated and cocked into position. The sound of M.A.F.A.R. saying all was clear put Norcotic in motion as he crept towards the back of the Mansion.

Norcotic would have never gone into this mission without seeing firsthand what he was facing, so every time he sent Sincere out to plan for the layout, he followed. It was not that he did not trust Sincere; he just wanted to catch whatever Sincere missed. It was a good thing he did because Sincere never checked the back of the Mansion. Looking at the Mansion from the front view, one would think that the two guards walking around the house would come around on different sides respectively covering both sides of the fortress in about five minutes. The truth is actually the reverse; the guards would walk around the sides of the Mansion but would have to turn back around due to the backyard being a sixty-foot cliff dropping into the James River. Therefore, watching from the front and seeing the guards cross each other from different directions would give the illusion that they were making a full rotation around the Mansion. Sincere missed this observation, but having studied their movements, Norcotic noticed the obvious. If the guards were to make a full rotation their positions would never switch, but by them having to stop on the sides of the Mansion and reverse their steps, they would leave one side facing east, and then come from the other side facing west.

The governor's biggest mistake was not having snipers on the roof because that would have been the only prevention keeping experienced intruders out. Norcotic made his way towards the edge of the cliff in the wooded area without being spotted and found what he was looking for. After realizing that he would have to scale the Mansion over the cliff, Norcotic knew he had left the proper equipment hidden in the woods after one of his stakeouts. Inside the black duffle bag was a hook and rope that he threw and it planted itself right on the balcony of the master bedroom which overlooked the James River. With the rope in place, Norcotic climbed the Mansion with the expertise of and experienced mountain climber scaling the Mansion for revenge.

Governor Douglas Wilber stood in his massive bedroom, which was decorated in the most expensive manner. Plush would have been and understatement. The most famous designers money could buy garnished the room. Douglas Wilber was dressed in silk boxers and an open robe exposing flabby flesh. He stared disapprovingly into a full body mirror wishing he could buy a new appearance. Sadly, there were some things that money couldn't purchase and in Doug's case that would be good looks.

It was now 2003 and he was very aware that he no longer possessed the looks he once had fourteen years ago. His belly protruded over his silk boxers, which made the sexy fabric seem everything but enticing. His grey hair reminded him of his father who said he would never amount to anything. As if reading his mind, Judge Snuckles-Wilber, his wife, crawled out of bed and seductively walked toward her husband with the intention of encouraging the man in her life.

"Ummm Tiger, are you going to stand there looking at that sexy body of yours or are you going to get your handsome self over here and give mommy some action?" Snuckles stood with her hands on her hips in a way that made the lingerie that graced her body appeal to more than just the head on a man's shoulders, but the other one as well.

Hearing his wife compliment him, and then seeing her attractive stance made him think of naughty things and apparently, his penis was thinking the same thing. His wife boosted his ego tremendously making him suck in his belly, giving him an instant tummy tuck as he gave her a devilish grin.

It had been a while since the couple had a gratifying moment together and tonight seemed like the perfect night. Snuckles-Wilber crawled into bed and rolled onto her back opening her legs seductively for her mate, who walked over eagerly to his prize. Lying on top of his wife, he kissed her with the hunger of a starving Ethiopian kid with a fried chicken wing; she returned his kisses with the same passion. Before things could get any hotter, Judge Snuckles-Wilber suddenly jumpedbup, pushing the governor off her steaming body. Feeling confused by his wife's reaction, Doug asked her, "Is something wrong, sweetie?"

"No dear, everything is fine, honey. I just remembered, I sent the chefs home for the weekend and I put a casserole in the oven that will burn this house down before we do if I don't turn the oven off. I'll be right back, dear," she replied, leaving the governor with soft emotions and a hard on.

After watching his wife leave the room, he made sure she was gone by listening to her footsteps pound away at the steps. Then Doug frantically raced around the room setting the mood for a scene that was only made for love making, looking like a set right out of a Ginuwine video shoot. Candles were being lit, fragrance was being sprayed in the air, and the music was being prepped to blast out of his brand new, state-of-the-art stereo system.

Within seconds, the sounds of Teddy Pendergrass filled the room becoming the cherry on top of this lustful cake. In the middle of his prepping, Doug heard a sound coming from his balcony, like that of metal being scraped against glass. As he walked towards the sliding glass door, Teddy belted sensual lyrics that filled the room.

"Turn off the lights and light a candle."

Doug opened the sliding door and stepped onto the balcony, but he saw nothing but a few birds nesting on the railing of the balcony. Unaware of the danger, he stepped back into his bedroom, closed the door behind him and slowly danced to the music.

Doug walked over to his secret stash behind his mini bar and poured himself a shot of Hennessy. The drink burned his chest making him close his eyes momentarily as it left a trail of fire down his throat. Doug's eyes being shut gave Norcotic the opportunity to creep up behind his enemy. Doug never saw Norcotic creep into his bedroom from the balcony, and it was a mistake that would cost him dearly. The governor opened his eyes, not knowing Norcotic was behind him.

"Turn off the lights," Norcotic sang into the governor's ear in time with the song, which got an approving response from the governor.

"Wow! These new surround sound speakers are out of fucking sight!"

That was when the governor felt the cold steel being pressed into the back of his head, which gave him an automatic brain freeze.

"Naw nigga, turn off the lights for real, pussy! Or I'll blast your nasty thoughts all over your out-of-shape body," Norcotic demanded.

The governor gulped down a nervous spit as Norcotic grabbed his walkie-talkie and screamed, "GO!"

Waiting for the signal in the woods, which surrounded the Mansion, Killa, E-Youngin, Sincere, and Ice sat eager to hear the word that would give them all a reason to start squeezing. But after twenty minutes, they were starting to get nervous.

"Yo, do y'all think he got in?" E-Youngin asked in a calm voice.

"You know that nigga in there," Ice replied. "But if he doesn't call on this radio in a minute I'm gonna bust this gauge off in this bitch." Killa was holding and AK-47 with a pineapple grenade waiting to hear the word.

Since Killa moved from Miami to Virginia, Norcotic had been by his side. Killa remembered being the new person in the neighborhood feeling the pain of an outcast and being rejected. Norcotic could have never said anything at all but when they crossed paths, he spoke.

"Bruh, you the new dude around here, right? Well this my hood, you with us, homeboy, aight?"

Every day after that, friends, women, and acceptance were plentiful. Respect was earned, but with Norcotic stamping Killa, it was all good. So, for Norcotic, anything was a green light, especially when there was money involved.

Life must have been anticipating the situation because every man was left to his own thoughts. The stillness of the moment made the men seem like statues unaware of the movements the world around them created. Even the word that came through the walkie-talkie appeared to have come out in slow motion.

"GO!"

They heard Norcotic's southern sound, and Killa looked over to Ice for the ready. A nod from the head of Ice got the team psyched. Killa pulled the pin from the grenade and launched the bomb towards the security guards.

The bomb flew like a football towards a sprinting wide receiver ready to score a touchdown in the Super Bowl. Killa's Brett Favre impersonation deserved and MVP because as soon as the grenade landed, the guards had no time to react.

BOOM!

In the midst of smoke and debris being blown about, you could actually make out body parts being ripped from torsos and tossed towards the sky. The two rotation guards, Albert and Smith, ran from their walking posts to examine the cause of the commotion. The other four guards stood with guns drawn, waiting for the smoke to clear.

Albert and his brother, Amir, were born in Mexico. Their parents sacrificed so much for them to live a normal life, but things were bad in the slums of Mexico. They made plans to walk through the desert and into America to give their children a better life. The extreme temperature of the desert claimed the life of the boys' mother. She would not drink any water in order to give the boys more water to avoid dehydration. The hiking was difficult, but they made it only because when Border Patrol came to seize the illegal immigrants, the boys' father diverted the authorities' attention while the boys ran for freedom. They watched as their father was detained and deported screaming the whole time.

"Albert, you make sure you take care of your little brother, no matter what!"

The boys grew up homeless, but Albert always looked out for Amir. As they got older and grew into men, they got a stroke of luck and ended up with government jobs working security. Douglas Wilber knew about the boys being in the United States illegally, but he never turned them in. He figured, why not have illegal aliens on his squad when going to make illegal deals with criminals. Albert and Amir just remained loyal and worked their way up to positions in the Governor's Mansion.

The smoke from the explosion was starting to evaporate giving everybody a better view of the wreckage. Sincere, a professional sniper, used the moment of chaos and calamity as a distraction to take out some guards. He wasted no time using his Sniper Rifle to pluck off as many targets as he could.

Swoop! Swoop!

Two guards dropped to the ground creating an uproar amongst the other guards as they scrambled for protection. Albert was pissed the fuck off! All his life he was his brother's keeper and, in the blink of an eye, a silent bullet traveled from the unknown and planted itself into his brother's eye socket before flying out of the back of his head. Amir was dead!

Having run from his walking post to the front of the mansion after hearing the explosion, Albert made it just in time to see his brother's death.

"You! Run upstairs and protect the governor! You! Come with me to battle these cocksuckers, they've killed my brother!" Albert screamed at the top of his lungs and none of the other guard challenged the head of security's decisions.

Ice was in murder mode from a rush of adrenaline he received from watching the bodies get blown apart.

"Hell yeah! That's what the fuck I'm talking about!" Ice yelled, cocking his shotgun and giving out orders. "Sincere, you, and Killa stay here and snipe everything you see moving. If it cannot be sniped, blow that shit up. E-Youngin, you with me so let's go!"

E-Youngin followed Ice gripping his Assault Rifle ready to spray some shit. As they reached the dead bodies, one of the victims was attempting to crawl away, only to have Ice put a slug in his cranium.

POW! POW! POW!

Unexpectedly like some sort of magic trick, two guards walking towards the wreck spotted the two men dressed in all black from head to toe, not revealing their identities and holding weapons of destruction. The guards assumed they must have been responsible for the violence. There was an injured guard crawling away feeling unbearable pain after having his leg blown completely off from his thigh. As he crawled, blood poured from his leg and his tear-stained face showed only turmoil. Albert already lost the life of his brother so saving any person was his mission at this point, even if they would live with only one leg.

One of the masked men walked up to the unarmed guard who was crawling legless and raised his shotgun while never taking his eyes off Albert.

"You don't have to kill him he's—" Before Albert could finish his negotiation, the masked man raised his shotgun high up the guard's body and blew his head clean off his shoulders. This was about more than protecting the governor now, this was flat out war, and Albert promised himself he would not lose. Bullets erupted from each man's gun as they aimed to kill their enemy while dodging bullets so not to end up like their prey.

"You killed my brother you son of a bitch!" Albert, the head of security, screamed out. BLOAW! BLOAW! BLOAW!

Ice tried his best not to become a corpse while shooting and yelling back, "Oh, that was your brother, which one? The pussy I shot in the eye? I bet he did not see it coming. Or was it the standup guy with no legs?" Ice laughed while sending buck shots at Albert.

"You are a bitch!" Albert screamed over gunshots immediately calling out to the intruder to put the guns down and fight him like a man. Albert dropped his gun and came out of cover. Ice saw this opportunity and approached Albert with his shotgun drawn, ready to shoot.

"Either you stupid or crazy as a motherfucker, so which is it?" Ice asked the guard.

"Neither," Albert said, "But you're a pussy because you won't fight me."

"Nope!" Ice said, pulling the trigger on the shotgun hoping to pop his top, but the loud click indicated that there were no more shells in the shotgun. This made Albert madder than he was before, and he rushed the masked man at full speed.

The other guard was in a heated shootout with the other

masked man who was shooting an AR-15, which seemed to never run out of bullets. The masked man had him pinned down and he was in no shape to try and help his friend until he killed his current nemesis. Ice was laughing so hard that he never noticed Albert running full speed towards him. It was too late. The guard tackled Ice like Goldberg, which caused him to drop the shotgun he was holding; they both went crashing down to the ground. Albert went from wrestling to boxing, raining blows on top of Ice, punch after punch. Both men knew the shotgun was nearby, and they fought hard trying to keep the other one from getting to the weapon. Albert tried his best to keep Ice from reaching the 12-gauge first, because even though it was not loaded, Ice could still use the shotgun like a bat or quickly reload the gun. Ice was determined to get to the shotgun, so he could blow the guard's face off, but not because there was a possibility he could die right now; it was the fact that he was getting his ass whopped! Reaching blindly for the shotgun, Ice felt something long, hard, and heavy.

Knowing that this was his shotgun, Ice gained incredible confidence and started swinging the weapon like a lunatic. The guard became terrified and jumped to his feet grabbing the shotgun Ice thought he had. Seeing Albert holding the shotgun got Ice's attention fast! He looked down at his hands wondering what he was holding. What he thought was the shotgun was actually a bloody leg.

"I'm going to kill you like you killed my brother!" Albert said, cocking the 12-gauge pump, chambering a non- existing shell. He forgot that the gun was empty.

"Hold on, my man. Legs talk about this for a minute," Ice replied, still in his comedy mood.

"FUCK YOU!" Albert screamed, busting an empty gun as Ice shut his eyes waiting for the slug to bust his melon.

"911, what's your emergency?" The operator spoke waiting to hear the cry for help on the other end of the phone.

"We are being attacked! Please send the police!" The guard who sent the call to the police was out of breath from running but managed to get the words out of his mouth.

"What is the address?" The operator asked.

"The Governor's Mansion," was all he said before hanging up the call and running back to join the gunfight.

E-Youngin was heavily under fire from the other guard's artillery forcing him to using the control booth by the gate as bulletproof protection. There was broken glass in and around the booth from the shattered windows of the structure looking like a broken heart. This gave E-Youngin an idea. Crawling like a marine doing war drills, E-Youngin made it safely inside the battered building to scoop a piece of glass off the floor. It was big enough to use as a third eye. Time in prison has given E-Youngin the talent of utilizing a mirror to spy on enemies and he planned to use that talent right now. E-Youngin placed the glass on the floor at an angle that gave him a clear reflection of his gun happy adversary.

Using the infrared beam attachment assembled on his AR-15, he aimed the beam at the glass, which then ricocheted and reflected light in the guard's eye temporarily blinding him. The moment of glitch in the guard's performance gave E-Youngin the chance to take advantage while the guard was recovering from blindness. Springing into action, E-Youngin jumped up and caught a bullet in the chest while returning fire, killing his opponent. The bulletproof vest he wore deflected the round from the now deceased shooter, but the shot still hurt like hell. Taking his mind off the bruise he would surely receive from the shot, E-Youngin was just in time to see Ice about to have his face pushed back.

When death becomes you, it is as if death flashes before your eyes. The sky opens revealing angels floating, and your brain releases memories of the past, which were long forgotten, but Ice did not witness any of that. With his eyes closed anticipating death, all he heard was a loud...

BANG!

Ice nearly jumped his skeleton out of his skin to expose the inner workings of a man. Expecting to see the devil himself, because there was no way he was making it into heaven, Ice slowly opened his eyes, letting out a sigh of relief after seeing E-Youngin standing over Albert's dead body. Ice filled with joy immediately and thought of Will Smith in *Bad Boys*.

"Now that's how you drive! From now on, that's how you drive!" he said.

"Yo! Tighten up, son," E-Youngin replied sternly, not being one to joke around.

"Fuck you, sucka! I could have handled that desert walking, wall hopping, flat faced spic on my own!" Ice spat, picking up his shotgun, loading a shell only to blast a hole in an already dead body. "Bitch!"

E-Youngin shook his head slowly at the spectacle Ice made as the boom from the shot echoed throughout the compound. Ice looked at E-Youngin and kicked Albert's corpse for good measure before saying, "Now let's go get this money!"

Spoken with true conviction, those were the words that propelled both men into the Mansion.

In all his fifteen years in office as the first black Governor of Virginia, Douglas Wilber never encountered anyone brave enough to break into his home. Knowing he had the best security money could buy, not to mention, two trained killers, Albert and Amir, out on the grounds, the governor was overly confident that this intruder would meet his maker.

"Boy! You have no idea who you are fooling with. I will have your head on a pl—" Douglas started.

BOOM!

The explosion that rocked the Mansion pushed Douglas' words back in his throat sending the man into a coughing rage.

"Shut the fuck up and stand straight, pussy!" Norcotic screamed, smacking the governor with the pistol. Now the governor was worried. Once Doug regained his composure, he yelled in a stentorian tone trying to alert his wife that there was trouble, "What the hell is going on here?"

"Motherfucker, I'm about two seconds away from turning your old ass into chicken grease. I'll be asking the fucking questions around here," Norcotic threatened, placing the barrel of both Desert Eagles directly into the governor's eyes.

"You have no idea who you're messing with, boy!" Doug laughed outlandishly.

"Yeah, I know, you told me that before," Norcotic replied, staring bug-eyed at the governor behind his ski mask, "I know exactly who I'm dealing with, pussy!"

Norcotic stepped so close to Governor Douglas Wilber's face that with every inhale, he could taste the fear served gourmet style on his taste buds.

"You're the same cunt that's responsible for my father being incarcerated while my mother had to raise me and my sister alone. We struggled and suffered in the streets. Yeah bitch! I know exactly who I'm fucking with, but do you know who you are dealing with, huh?"

This made Douglas Wilber scared as hell because now he knew this matter was personal and that he still had no idea who was standing in his bedroom holding two guns at his head. The masked man continued with his threats.

"It's me, Doug. Block! In the flesh."

Douglas stumbled backwards trying to escape the nightmare he apparently stepped into, but to no avail. He fell on the floor and tried to crawl under the bed, but Norcotic was too quick. He pulled the frantic man, who was now crying, back into the open. Doug had literally shitted his pants with the reality that Block was now in his home and the whole room now smelled like a truck stop Porta Potty.

Douglas Wilber turned white as a bag of Columbian nose candy, and he honestly thought a ghost long buried had come to take him to the underworld. Hearing the name Block had brought back memories he had abandoned years ago. It was as if the past was coming back to haunt his future.

"Please don't kill me; take whatever you want. You can have it all, even my wife! I mean she's a lousy cook but hey, she could suck a golf ball out of a Hole in One," Doug pleaded.

The governor was crying snot from his nose as Norcotic stood examining the situation as it unfolded.

"Man don't nobody want that wrinkled up pussy you call a wife! Fuck all that! I want the pictures, videos, and the $500,000 in cash you owe my father!" Norcotic roared, slapping the governor in the face with his open fist.

"Ouch!" Douglas Wilber yelled, rubbing his cheek where Norcotic had just slapped the fire out of him, "Your father?" he asked out of confusion.

"Yeah nigga, my father! Block is my Pops, nigga."

An expression of relief washed over the governor's face as he thought the worst of the worst, is not happening, but there was still and angry boy holding two pistols standing in his room. He decided to toy around.

"What pictures and money are you talking about, boy?" Doug shouted trying to play stupid with the gunman, which earned him a bullet that broke his big toe.

BLOCKA!

"Aruuuugh!" Douglas Wilber screamed in agony, holding his foot, while rolling around over the floor trying to extinguish a fire covering him.

"Now keep playing with me and the rest of those Little Piggy's won't make it into any more nursery rhymes!" Norcotic fumed.

"Alright, ALRIGHT!" The governor complied, "Just please don't shoot."

At that moment, Norcotic's sixth sense alerted him to the presence of an unwanted guest.

"Oh my God, am I glad to see you," Douglas said, still holding his bleeding foot.

Norcotic turned around faster than bad karma only to receive some as he stared into a big gun, and the eyes of an unexpected security guard. After making a call to the Richmond City Police Department, Johnson, the last surviving guard, rushed to protect the governor, and obviously showed up just in time. With the weapon drawn and pointed at Norcotic's head, all the masked intruder could do was pass over the guns and hope his team would save his life.

Judge Snuckles-Wilber was roaming around in her kitchen, lost in a world of lust as she prepared to take her casserole out of the oven. She glanced out of the kitchen window and noticed that there seemed to be a rope leading to her bedroom balcony. This was odd for the fact that there was no backyard, just a cliff, and over the ledge, a raging river. The judge opened the window to confirm her suspicion, and soon her concern for the worst arrived. There was suddenly a loud explosion that ripped through the air like wet paper being torn, with gunfire immediately following the eruption. Screaming for her life, Judge Snuckles-Wilber dove under the kitchen table frightened. Her reaction would have reminded one of a kid covering their head with a blanket to hide from the boogeyman. Her first thought was of the family she would never see again; her second thought was of her husband.

Thinking of her husband gave her the motivation to be brave, and make sure her husband was alright. When she crawled from out of the cover of her kitchen table, two masked men greeted the judge. One was holding a shotgun, and the other had an Assault Rifle. Mrs. Snuckles-Wilber stood there as if she were a deer in the headlights of a Mack truck, and her fear only prompted the men to create more havoc.

"Ummm! Would you look at this; this bitch done got all sexy for me. I'm going to have fun fucking you in the ass with my shotgun," Ice said while using the gun as a prop for his dick. He started to stroke the barrel like a hard penis. The judge turned and started to sprint faster than a Sonic and Roadrunner race only to be tripped up by E-Youngin's AR-15 clipping her ankles.

"Where the fuck you think you going, bitch?" E-Youngin said while wrestling with Judge Snuckles-Wilber, who was fighting frantically while the masked man ripped her lingerie exposing milky white breasts and hard strawberry colored nipples.

"Noooo! Somebody please help me!" Judge Snuckles-Wilber screamed only to hear that damn Teddy Pendergrass music taunt her plea.

"Let me give you what you've been waiting for," Teddy sang through the speakers, and that was exactly what E-Youngin was trying to give her, what she had been waiting for. Ice had made himself at home by getting a plate of the casserole and stuffing his mouth, while enjoying the porn of E-Youngin raping the judge.

"Damn this is some good ass casserole, Mrs. Judge Lady. Hey, do you think I can fix a plate to go?" he asked her.

The only reply the judge could muster was a few moans from the big dick ripping her pussy walls to pieces.

"Urrgghh, urggghhh!" she screamed, only to make Ice mad.

"You are so rude; I asked you a question, but it's okay, I've had better casserole anyway," Ice replied.

After watching E-Youngin nut all over the judges face, Ice rubbed the barrel of the shotgun in Crisco and rammed it deep into the women's anus so hard that blood splattered on the floor.

"Eeeewwww! Is that blood or shit?" E-Youngin asked.

"I don't know," Ice replied, "Let's make her lick it."

The judge was near unconsciousness so when Ice rubbed her face into the bloody feces, there was no rebuttal. After her meal of unwanted shit and blood, the masked men began dragging her towards the master bedroom. She blacked out before reaching the hallway.

Back in the master bedroom, Norcotic was in the Full Nelson wrestling move by the guard that he now knew was named Johnson. Doug Wilber took out his frustration by delivering blows to Norcotic's midsection while he was rendered helpless. With each punch, he screamed with emphasis, "You break," he said and landed a blow to Norcotic's ribs, "into my house," he paused to deliver another punch, "and demand," he hit Norcotic twice before saying, "MONEY!"

The guard watched Norcotic drop to the floor and gasp for air.

"Tie him to a chair," were the orders given by the governor. "We're going to make him wish he never stormed onto my property."

Amid the destruction in the master bedroom, the door opened and in stepped Snuckles-Wilber with a ton of C4 duct taped to her chest. She was naked, with shit and blood stuck to her legs like flies on a discarded cheeseburger. Not knowing what to do, Johnson aimed his gun at the two masked men who came in after the judge. That was enough time to give Norcotic the advantage he needed. Using the gift of divine intervention, Norcotic swiftly overpowered the guard with a leg sweep that sent Johnson crashing to the ground and his gun in the air. In one motion, Norcotic jumped up, grabbed the gun, and came down with a military roll, stopping with the gun pointed at the governor.

He spotted his two twin Desert Eagles and traded the guard's gun for them. Governor Doug Wilber was in a daze seeing his wife bloody and strapped to a bomb. Never in a million years would he have pictured this scene transpiring here today.

"By the way I had to push the barrel of this shotgun deep in her tight little asshole. It's obvious that you ain't been fucking her right. With your little ass pencil dick!" Ice said breaking the silence, while Judge Snuckles-Wilber began to cry.

The governor became aroused with devious emotions, and he charged at the masked men only to be stopped by a couple of bullets from Norcotic's guns popping him in the legs.

As Sincere and Killa sat waiting for their next orders, they became aware of police car sirens blaring in the distance getting closer and closer.

"Killa, do you hear that?" Sincere asked, receiving a head nod in response.

"I think we might have company."

While Killa placed the grenades on the ground to grab the walkie-talkie, he heard the crack of Sincere's Sniper Rifle.

"Damn, another one?" Killa asked.

"Yeah, I think that's it though; he just came running out of the house," Sincere replied.

This prompted Killa to radio Ice and see what the hell was going on.

"Yo Ice! We got the boys in blue coming our way. What do you want us to do? Are we still sniping and blowing shit up?"

After a few seconds, Ice came in.

"Norcotic said come inside and meet us in the master bedroom. Do not leave any signs of our whereabouts!" Ice informed them and Sincere and Killa made their way into the Mansion.

Ice got off the radio with Killa and Sincere and saw that Norcotic and E-Youngin had finished tying up the judge and Johnson to the bed. Ice then hit Douglas Wilber in the face and put the shotgun to the head of his wife.

"Now this is going to be my last time asking you, old man," Ice said, removing the gun from Judge Snuckles-Wilber's head and sliding it into her swollen pussy. "If you don't open this safe, I'm going to blow pussy all over this room; now what is the fucking combination?"

"Okay!" Douglas gave in.

After all that went down today, it was clear these people were professionals, and he need not cause his wife any more pain. The chances of them leaving this situation alive to retaliate were slim to none. That was quite clear by one of the masked men removing his ski mask and revealing his identity. Governor Douglas Wilber recognized him to be Block's son. Giving these men what they wanted was his only trump card in this dangerous deck, and what other choice did he have? The governor agreed, getting to his feet as best he could; he limped towards a large painting of himself counting money and smoking a Cuban cigar. He pulled at one of the bottom corners which swung back to reveal a large hidden safe. Within minutes, the governor had the safe open and he reached inside.

The governor turned around with two nine millimeters, blazing. Norcotic expected this sort of last desperate attempt of defiance and anticipated the rebellion. He quickly emptied both clips of his Desert Eagles into the governor's body until he lay in a pile of lifeless waste. Judge Snuckles-Wilber and Johnson wiggled in their restraints after seeing Norcotic smoke the governor, but to no avail. They knew they were next. With the safe open, Killa and Sincere arrived just in time to help Ice and E-Youngin empty the contents and prepare for the escape. Norcotic went through every drawer in the governor's adjoining office and could not find the pictures or videos he was looking for.

As he searched for the evidence, Sincere spoke up.

"Norcotic, the police are here. How are we going to get out of here? I saw the view from the kitchen window, we're above the James River, bruh! On a fucking cliff!"

As if on cue, the police started yelling over a bullhorn.

"We have the place surrounded, come out with your hands up, or we are coming in!"

Norcotic ignored both his team's and the police's concerns and threats with only one thing on his mind, the success of the mission. So far, his father, Block had been in prison for 16 years, and Norcotic could only imagine the pain of having those crackers tell you when to sleep, when to eat, when to take a shower, never having any privacy, and having to watch your back 24/7 all because you were blackmailed and set up. Norcotic began to search harder.

"Yo Norcotic!" Ice yelled after seeing his brother in crime continue to look for what did not want to be found.

"We got to go, bruh. Jail is not part of the plan, Nor."

Out of pure anger and frustration, Norcotic punched the wall of Douglas Wilber's room leaving a hole bigger than his fist inside the wall. The hole was so big that you could literally see through it, and they did. They saw right into the hidden room on the other side. With the speed of an angry boxer and

Jujitsu Master, the team of men started kicking and punching the wall until there was a hole big enough to squeeze through to the other side. Once inside, it only took Norcotic two minutes to find the pictures and videos needed to free his father from prison.

"This is your last warning, come out with your hands up! Or face heavy repercussions." The police were still making threats, but eventually they would follow up on their promises...

"They got helicopters!" Sincere exclaimed nervously.

Soon as he spoke, a bright spotlight flashed into the bedroom causing everyone to duck out of sight. Norcotic looked at his team, who all looked back as if to say "How the hell are we going to get out of this?"

"Does everybody know how to swim?" Norcotic smiled.

Time seems to go by fast when you are having fun, and to Sergeant Marshall, his job was more than fun; it was extremely exciting! There was a possible hostage situation at the Governor's Mansion, and from the looks of it, a possible homicide of a government official. There was no way that Marshall would have that on his watch, so his mind was strictly on the rescue of any individual he could save; if there was anyone to save. Time was flying, and after requesting, twice already, for the suspects to come out, unarmed, with their hands in the air, the squad had received no response. Sergeant Marshall could not believe the massacre he had seen outside. It had been years since anyone had seen a blood bath like the one they were walking through now.

Once they were on the third floor, the tactical team stopped in front of the master bedroom doors. With one hard kick, the police came crashing into the bedroom and what they saw shocked them all speechless. The honorable Judge Snuckles-Wilber was tied to the bed with a shotgun stuffed so far up her pussy that the shells were fertilizing her eggs. The security guard had his head completely sawed off his neck, and Governor Douglas Wilber was filled with so many bullet holes, if he would have drank water, he would have looked like a human cloud on a rainy day. What had grabbed everybody's attention almost immediately was what had been written on the wall in blood.

GO HARD OR GO HOME!

On further inspection, all three of the dead bodies had "M'Z UP" carved onto their stomachs and chests. Sergeant Marshall knew this was the workings of M.A.F.A.R. MAFIA.

"Hey! Somebody get on the phone and call the captain. Tell him M.A.F.A.R. MAFIA is behind this."

One of the officers was ready to follow the orders given by the sergeant until he noticed an awkward bag sitting by the dead bodies. He looked inside and when the sergeant saw his actions, Marshall screamed, "Do not tamper with evidence!" his demand went unheard with what had been discovered inside the bag.

"IT'S A REALLY BIG FUCKING BOMB!"

All the officers ran from the room in a confused panic, but not a soul would make it out alive.

Norcotic was the first one to come up for air, followed by Ice, Killa, Sincere, and finally E-Youngin.

"Here! Assemble this!" Norcotic said, handing E-Youngin a bag filled with parts for a disposable rocket launcher. The mission had been a success so far, and with the money, pictures, and videos in tow, it was now time for the fireworks.

"Yo, E-Youngin, you got one shot. Blow that fucking bird out the sky!" Norcotic said while diving underwater. Sincere, Ice, and Killa followed as E-Youngin aimed and sent a missile towards the spotlight that was shining on their location.

BAM!

The helicopter burst into about a thousand tiny pieces. Coming up for air, the team watched as debris from the chopper landed angrily in the river almost adding to the danger of drowning.

"Yeeeaaahhhh!" The team screamed seeing the mission was turning out in their benefit. The guys floated in the dangerous water, savoring the moment of victory.

"Yo, Norcotic, I almost died on the zip line, nigga!" Killa said, spitting water out of his mouth. Nobody but Norcotic knew they would end up in the powerful currents on the James River, and he was prepared for the escape.

"You think that's wild, well check this out," Norcotic pulled a remote from his swimsuit while the last member was stepping out of the water onto dry land. He pressed the button and…KABOOOOM!

The Mansion exploded into a huge, bright light, killing everything inside. Before leaving the Mansion on the zip line, Norcotic removed the C-4 from Judge Snuckles- Wilber and placed the bombs inside of a duffle bag. He figured if the police saw the bomb on her, they would exit the Mansion and call the bomb squad. This ensured that about the time they got to land, he would be able to get rid of everyone inside. No witnesses, no evidence, no case.

The team shouted joyfully, celebrating so loud you

would've thought someone just won a gold medal at the Olympics. The sounds of victory overcame the moment like an owl over a mouse when Sincere asked, "So, what's next?"

Ice and Norcotic replied at the same damn time, "The world is next, nigga! That's what's next!"

CHAPTER 2

III

"Build and Destroy"

Block was in his maximum-security cell working out as usual, but today, his workout was harder than normal. Whenever something was on his mind, there were only three things that could get everything back in order. One was pussy but being that he was in a super max facility, that would never happen. The second thing was to kill somebody, but being locked down 23 hours a day, every day, made that difficult. And even in the one hour he got, why kill someone when there were bigger fish to fry? The last alternative was to work out and relieve stress, but when a person had worked out every day for 16 years, they become bored as hell!

It had been a year since Block had spoken to his son about the evidence that could set him free. Having patience was something that being incarcerated instilled into a man. Whether they wanted it or not. But at the end of the day, a man is only human, and Block was getting to his boiling point. After every set of push-ups, which was a hundred and fifty a set with him now on his 26th set, Block would punch the wall and yell out whatever came to his mind.

"I will kill Hitler and shit in his mouth! Fuck the whole world and cum in the core of the Earth!"

PUNCH! PUNCH! PUNCH!

"Dead bodies all over my nut sack you sensitive bitch! I can't wait to kill one of these prison guards with my toothbrush!"

He was hitting the wall so hard, and so many times that his hands were swollen. He had put permanent dents in the cement from punching it.

"Motherfucka, I will kill all of you motherfuckas! Right here and right, NOW!"

Block was losing his mind, and no matter what the staff said or threatened him with, there was no stopping the killer. This had now been going on for close to two hours.

The officers were only hoping to calm Block down. They knew there was nothing they could do about the situation. The last time an officer tried to stop Block from venting, Block broke the officer's neck and was on 24-hour lock for 4 years. Standing in his cell with his fists balled up so tight, the knuckles on his hand threatened to pop out like Janet Jackson's titties at the Super Bowl. Block walked around the cell huffing and puffing like a crazy bull. Soon as his temper was about to reach an extremely dangerous level, Block's television aired a story about Governor Douglas Wilber being assassinated along with his wife, Judge Snuckles-Wilber. A smile spread across Block's face, but one would have thought he was still frowning.

The officers, no longer hearing the commotion, ran down to Block's cell to see if everything was okay. Finally, reaching the doors of his cell and looking through the shatterproof glass, the officers found Block standing in his cell motionless.

"Hey Block! Are you alright, buddy?"

Block never replied. Several more attempts only resulted in the same results, so the officer left and assigned a guard to Block's cell to make sure he did not kill himself. It was crazy how suicide was the only escape for some people in this hellhole, but the D.O.C. would do whatever they could to keep a person from killing themselves. If the D.O.C. was not responsible for killing an inmate, they damn sure wanted you to do every single day of your sentence in that piece of shit they call a prison.

Once the captain came to do his rounds, he asked the officer if Block was still causing trouble.

"No sir, he's actually been doing really well!"

"Really well you say? Are we talking about the same person, officer?" The captain could not believe someone had said that Block was doing really well, but he knew that the officer guarding Block's cell was well experienced.

"What exactly has he been doing?" asked the captain "Nothing, he's just been standing there."

The captain looked into the cell and saw that Block was just standing there with an evil grin on his face. The look worried the captain, but he knew asking Block what was wrong would get no results, so he asked the officer.

"How long has he been standing there like that, officer?"

The officer calculated the numbers in his head before he answered, "Umm, he's been standing there since before the beginning of my shift, so it's safe to say he hasn't moved from that spot in 6 or 7 hours, sir."

The captain just shook his head.

Out of breath and running for his life, Norcotic advanced through what seemed like a maze in the form of a four- story project in the ghetto of an unknown city. The night was very dark without a star in the sky to illuminate the streets below. It was the kind of dark that death wished had some light. Taking the time to look around, and scope his surroundings out, Norcotic wiped away perspiration. It had begun to slide from his forehead down to his face. There was no way to tell if the discharge came from the night's muggy weather, or from the nervousness he felt knowing there was a possibility that he could die tonight. In his hand was a semi-automatic and his only thought was to complete the mission's objective and murder the leader of the opposition.

Norcotic's team consisted of Legion, Ice's younger brother. Legion was a little darker where Ice was light in complexion. Even though he was younger, Legion was taller than Ice at 6'3, and highly intelligent. Legion was enrolled as a US Marine, and every time he came back home he had amazing stories to tell the squad. Killa was also on Norcotic's team. Killa was new to M.A.F.A.R., but ever since Norcotic met him he knew there was something about the Miami native, and he proved to be right. Killa was a hustling motherfucker and when there was money involved, he was a complete animal.

To complete the team was Sincere. Sincere along with Ice were the pimps of the crew, but whereas Ice was the gangster, Sincere was the total opposite, respectful and very polite. However, it would be a deadly mistake to get his manners confused with weakness, because he was a silent killer. Ice's team was the group at which the war was being fought against, and Norcotic wanted them all dead!

Ice's team consisted of Tiny, who was 6 feet and 6 inches tall. A straight monster of a man; one would rather meet a hungry bear than Tiny. E-Youngin was Ice's next member hailing from Queens, New York, so he brought a humble vibe to Ice's team of reckless, violent members. Then there was Mouse, the only one in the crew who was not a killer. Out of the eight men, only Tiny and Norcotic were born and raised in Richmond, VA with Tiny being from the west end and Norcotic from the Southside. Ice and his brother, Legion, were both from Newark, NJ. Sincere, E-Youngin, and Mouse were from New York with Sincere being from Brownsville, Mouse from Flatbush, and E-Youngin was from Queens.

Collectively, the men made up the gang known as M.A.F.A.R. MAFIA. M.A.F.A.R. is an acronym that stands for, My Artificial Family Always Rydes. The guys really lived by the motto, and they all vowed to never let anything come in between them. Since the day they all met, the boys were hard to separate, and they always had each other's backs. The squad was not like most men in a gang. They saw themselves as an organization, and there was structure within the ranks to control authority even though they all were bosses. Ice was the general and Legion was only a soldier. They moved to Richmond, VA after their father died. Rumor had it that their father was a high-ranking gang leader whose body was found chopped to pieces in a suitcase. When their mother went to go to work, she discovered the suitcase and what was inside. She packed up her family and moved A.S.A.P.

The second highest rank belongs to the Major Norcotic. Killa was the captain, Tiny was the sergeant, Sincere and E-Youngin were both lieutenants, and Mouse was the commander. One thing grouped all these men together and that was hard times. Money was always the motive, and to get it how you lived required practice.

Norcotic resumed a running pace, dressed in army fatigues, compliments of Legion stealing clothes and equipment whenever he was on base; Norcotic was trying to find Ice and put a hole in his head before Ice found him and did the same.

Sincere must have read Norcotic's mind because he came over the radio with some great intel.

"Major, I can see Ice in the scope of my weapon. He is on the top floor of building 3655. Do you want me to take him out?

"Naw, I got him; it ain't nothing!" Norcotic replied.

Knowing that he was currently in building 3659, Norcotic knew he had a few obstacles in between him and his target, but he made his move. It would prove to be a tough mission because only Norcotic and Sincere stood alive on his team, and now, Sincere was only being used as a lookout. There were also two alive on Ice's team, E-Youngin and the general himself.

"Norcotic, I spotted E-Youngin closing in on your Location," Sincere alerted through the radio.

"Let him come," Norcotic said, "He won't live to talk about it."

"I feel you, Nor," Sincere responded.

Waiting for a while, Norcotic got back on the radio and asked Sincere if he'd seen any signs of Ice since the last time he spotted him.

"Nope! It's like the man disappeared or something."

Norcotic's advantage at this point was the fact that E-Youngin had no clue that Norcotic knew he was on his way to his position. The only thing that bothered Norcotic was the fact that Ice was very sneaky.

Ice you are a very slick man, Norcotic thought as he made up his mind not to kill E-Youngin. He figured that was exactly what Ice wanted. If not, why send E-Youngin in the open like that when he knew that Norcotic would use Sincere's sniper skills to either kill E-Youngin or get the drop on his location. Norcotic chose to avoid E-Youngin and go after the general himself, and he'd let Sincere handle E-Youngin. Everybody knew in war that if you took the head, then the body would fall. With that in mind, Norcotic made his way to the fourth floor of building 3655 where Ice had last been seen. Looking from the fourth-floor vantage point, Norcotic tried to see if he could spot Ice, but only saw E-Youngin creeping back to building 3655. Norcotic crept to the landing on the staircase between the second and third floor and watched as E-Youngin ascended to the top using the opposite staircase.

Without being seen, Norcotic used the same stairs as E-Youngin, following him to the top floor and putting three bullets in his back.

POP! POP! POP!

E-Youngin was dead. Since Sincere was watching Norcotic's back through the scope, he never noticed Ice standing behind him with his weapon drawn. Ice wasted no time pushing his shit back. Hearing the death of Sincere over the radio pissed Norcotic off. He raced back over to Sincere's location hoping to see Ice along the way. He rounded a corner only to be stopped dead in his tracks by the barrel of Ice's gun.

The other six members of M.A.F.A.R. were around to see the scene play out in their game of manhunt using paintball guns. Norcotic portrayed Cain and Abel with the assistance of Ice.

Looking in each other's eyes, Norcotic quoted a line from *New Jack City.*

"Am I my brother's keeper?"

"Yes, I am!" Ice replied, and then he shot Norcotic three times in the head. BOOM!

Norcotic jumped awake from his dream of paintball wars to find he was surrounded by money, his crew, and a television blaring the news, which he had no clue his father was watching at the same time. It was the day after the robbery and the guys were counting their spoil and splitting the income into equal shares, while waiting to hear what the news would say about the heist.

"Aye Yo! You still having them bad dreams, son?" E-Youngin asked Norcotic, who had a look of bewilderment on his face.

"Yeah bruh, shit be wild as a bitch, shawdy" the sound of sleep still in Norcotic's voice, answered E-Youngin's question.

"Well sleep when you die, nigga! We just got $100,000 each, so you can pay for them little Freddy Krueger nightmares you be having, daydreaming, and shit," Ice said as he threw money in the air while he drunk Moet out of the bottle.

Norcotic just shook his head as he put his shoes back on and sat straight up on the sofa. He started getting his thoughts together for today because there was a lot to be done. Walking over to the kitchen, Norcotic made a quick turkey sandwich and wolfed it down so fast there was no way he tasted it. Norcotic then plopped down on the sofa and grabbed the remote, blasting 50 Cent's *Get Rich or Die Trying* through the speakers. Sincere got agitated and threw a box of dutches at Norcotic to get his attention.

"Shhh! The news is coming on, it's breaking news about the Mansion," he said while pointing to the television. "This is Juan Caunde with Fox News. There was an explosion last night at the Governor's Mansion that claimed the lives of numerous people. Included in the death toll was Governor Douglas Wilber, along with his wife, Judge Snuckles-Wilber. Members of the Richmond City Police Department's Tactical Force were also killed in what was being called an accidental explosion but is now being investigated as a murder. The explosion was so intense that investigators say any evidence was burned inside, but the search of the James River did turn up the canister that was used to hold an RPG missile. If you have any leads please call 1-800- CRIMESTOPPERS." Sincere turned off the television and there was a loud uproar from the brothers in crime.

"We did it!" Killa celebrated by turning up the Moet bottle and drinking the champagne like a rock star. Everybody was celebrating except Norcotic, who was looking at E-Youngin with menace in his eyes. If looks could kill, E-Youngin would have been as dead as a doorknob. With the speed of a rattlesnake, Norcotic jumped off the sofa and grabbed E-Youngin by the throat, squeezing the life from his lungs.

Everyone was trying to pull Norcotic off E-Youngin, who looked to be close to passing out. Before he blacked out, Norcotic stopped choking him.

"Why everybody celebrating and stunting for, huh!" he yelled.

"Just chill son, we just had a good mission; it's all good," Mouse tried to reason with Norcotic.

E-Youngin caught his wind and tried to rush Norcotic for a fight, but he was caught by Tiny. Smacking and kicking bottle off the coffee table sending Moet, money and weed flying everywhere, E-Youngin hollered at the top of his lungs.

"What the fuck is wrong with you, yo!"

"You, nigga! That's what the fuck is wrong with me. Your stupid ass, you dumb motherfucker. How in the hell you forget the canister after you fired the missile?" Norcotic asked.

"Norcotic, ain't nobody trying to hear that bullshit. You the one that got us neck deep in the wild ass James River trying to bust a fucking helicopter out the sky in the rapids. FUCK YOU!" E-Youngin replied.

Norcotic began gathering his share of the money, and the evidence he needed to free his pops. He knew it was time for him to leave before he killed one of his niggas.

"Well, if we get locked up don't forget, like E-Youngin forgot proof of our involvement, that his stupidity caused EVERYTHING!" Norcotic said preparing to leave. "I'm going to see my bitch, get at me though," he said walking towards the door.

Before he exited the hallway, Ice yelled after him.

"That sounds like a good idea, Nor, go fuck the shit out her ass and get that stress off your chest!"

They all laughed except E-Youngin, but Norcotic planned to take Ice's advice to the fullest.

Sitting in front of her vanity mirror combing her hair straight, Blu was admiring her features, which were a combination of her powerful parents' features. After taking a long, hot bath in warm milk and rose petals to relieve the tension while moisturizing her skin, Blu called her family once again only to receive no answer. This prompted Blu to prepare herself quickly to go over to her parents' house to see if they were all right. Normally, Blu would have spoken to at least one of her parents by now. She spoke to them every day, but obviously last night and today was not a good time for them to speak with their daughter.

Blu's delicate features and soft personality attracted many men who never knew her real occupation, which she lied about constantly. Blu was not even her real name. During off time, she was a normal girl, but on the job, she was the meanest federal agent in the field working for the FBI. Blu made it a ritual to call her parents daily, since they were government employees as well. With all the weirdos in the world who felt like when they broke the law it wasn't their fault, she worried about her parents. They took an oath to protect, judge, and uphold the law, so naturally they could be targeted. Blu made it a ritual to call her parents daily.

Hair combed and opting not to apply any make-up since she was only stepping out for a minute, her cell phone rang as soon as she grabbed her keys to leave. Thinking it was her mom or dad, she rushed to answer only to be upset by the voice of her commander on the other end.

"Hey, Hello Ciera, are you sitting down?"

"What! No, I am not sitting down. I'm actually on my way out of the house. What is wrong? Nobody calls someone and asks them are they sitting down, so what's up? Do you need me to come in?" Blu asked.

"No, no, it's nothing like that; it's just that…Have you seen the news today?" her commander asked.

"No, I haven't seen the news, Roger! You know I do not watch that. After all we face in one day, I don't come home and remind myself of the madness, unless I feel it can help a case in some way."

Roger now knew that this call would be harder than he expected. He wanted to tell her in person, but he knew that

Blu would totally lose it, and he wanted her to be home when she found out the information. Blu pushed for Roger to hurry along with the conversation.

"Okay, Roger, let's get to why you called, because like I said, I was on the way out to handle some personal business. I have to go see my mom and dad, so what's up?" she urged.

Roger knew there was no easy way to say it, so he would just have to do it.

"You were put on a case today, a 20-man homicide case, well a massacre really, but I immediately took you off when I realized that... Two of the victims were your parents."

Blu's heart dropped in her chest causing pain so unbearable that her whole body felt numb. Her cell phone dropped, mirroring what her heart had done inside her soul, and when her heart shattered, it mimicked the crack on her phone screen. Blu did not say a word, she dared not to, or she would cry her eyes out for sure.

"Hello! Hello!" Roger could be heard screaming to get Blu's attention not knowing that his attempts were falling on deaf ears.

Six minutes went by before Blu snapped out of her trance and picked up the phone. A few lonely tears escaped her eyes quietly as she viewed her cracked cell phone screen behind salty pain still making out that her phone was on.

"Hello?" she said, not remembering that Roger had called until she heard his voice and the memory rushed, flooding her with emotions all over again.

"Ciera, are you alright? I've called a team over to your house for Christ's sake. I didn't know if you were going to harm yourself or what!"

Half listening to her superior's rant, Blu demanded to be put back on the case.

"Now you know we can't do that; you are the best agent for the job but when we found out that you were related to..."

Blu ended the call, hanging up on Roger. She grabbed her service gun and car keys, heading to the only person who could put her back on the case.

Tra-8 was just getting out of a hot, steamy shower. She previously was at work and the lather helped wash away a day of sweat. Working the morning shift for the United States Post Office made her want to get the rest that she needed and deserved. Even though she had rest on her mind, the shower had her thinking about her man, Norcotic. Having a mental visual of her boyfriend got her lust flowing and her love dripping, making her wet between the thighs, and it had nothing to do with the water from the shower. Usually, Norcotic would come over for breakfast after her Uncle Rusty left the crib. He always wanted to avoid a confrontation when crossing Rusty's path because for some reason, Rusty hated Norcotic. Just the thought of everybody wanting to deny her what she wanted, made her clit throb for Norcotic more. The shower she took turned into a self-inflicted four-play.

Cumming all over her fingers somehow replaced thoughts of pleasure with feelings of neglect. It had been three days since she had seen Norcotic. He was a no show, and his cell phone kept going straight to voicemail. Tra-8 moved in with her Uncle Rusty in Richmond, VA from Crown Heights in Brooklyn, NY after her mother, Stacie, died, and the killer was still at large. If it weren't for her cousin, Day-Day, and her man, Norcotic, Tra-8 would have lost her mind living with her Uncle Rusty. Rusty had a record label by the name of G-

Fam Records, but on top of his business, he was the biggest cocaine supplier on the East Coast. Rusty dealt in the streets and did not like Tra-8 dealing with people that had the street mentality like Norcotic.

Rusty lost his sister, Stacie, to the ruthlessness of the game, and he vowed to make sure Tra-8 would not meet the same fate. Leaving the shower with Norcotic still on her mind, Tra-8 started to lotion herself in her bedroom. Her sanctuary was in the basement of Rusty's mansion. There was only one window in Tra-8's room, and that is where Norcotic was seated, spying on Tra-8 as she put on a private show; she had no idea she was performing. Tra-8 was cinnamon complexioned, lightly mixed with maple and brown sugar. Her jet-black hair fell like a waterfall to her slender, round shoulders having the tendency of making ghetto girls jealous.

She was 5'5 standing on long legs, and thick thighs that held a soft beautiful booty. She was all body! In addition, watching her lotion her body was a gift from heaven. Norcotic tapped on the window, and she knew it could only be her thoughts in the flesh. He waited for her to open the window, so he could climb inside. Once in the room, the two lovebirds hugged each other like they had been separated for years, just seeing one another again for the first time since splitting. Holding each other was the only way not to be separated again. Tra-8 noticed the duffle bag in Norcotic's hand, but never got the opportunity to question him about the bag because his Southern slur made her horny all over again.

"What's happening, shawty?"

"Nothing!" Tra-8 sung, stepping to Norcotic. She was standing on her tippy toes with her arms wrapped around his neck applying a soft kiss to his lips and making his dick super hard. She could feel the print of his penis pressing against her body through his denims. Tra-8's towel had fallen to the floor when she hugged Norcotic, finding a place right beside the duffle bag he placed on the floor. Her breasts, all 36C, filled with hard nipples brushed up against her man as they embraced driving him insane. They continued to kiss increasing the intensity by adding tongue, making their mouth do a dance that only they knew the music to. Norcotic sucked on her bottom lip and squeezed her ass causing Tra-8 to open her legs and climb into Norcotic's arms.

Suspended in the air now, their intimate moment felt like a magic carpet ride. When Norcotic put Tra-8 back down, she wasted no time squatting down to her knees, undoing Norcotic's belt, and pulling his pants down to his ankles releasing his phat dick from the confinement of his boxer shorts. While Tra-8 sucked the meat off his dick, Norcotic stepped out of his shoes and kicked off his jeans without his dick ever leaving the comfort of his woman's warm, wet, pistol pleasing lips. Tra-8 took all 8 inches of Norcotic's phat, circumcised dick deep in her mouth, slurping and spitting all over his manhood making it sloppy and nasty. Spit was dripping down onto her titties making her breasts really glossy.

"Yeah, nigga fuck my face! Fuck the shit out my pretty ass face! Make me shut the fuck up," Tra-8 said while jerking his dick and clapping her ass.

Norcotic slapped her on the ass and lifted her chin slightly coaching her on how to suck his dick.

"Aight baby, I'ma slow stroke your face, then ram my nut sack deep in your throat, and you better slurp that motherfucker hard as a bitch, you hear me!?"

Tra-8 responded by opening her mouth as wide as she

could inviting that big black pool stick to hit them balls in the side pocket. Norcotic fucked Tra-8's face like he was trying to break her neck, then unexpectedly he rammed his meat deep in her mouth causing her to rise up off her knees choking on the dick in her throat. Norcotic held her head in placed and yelled, "Bitch, breathe through your nose, and you better not bite me!"

Tra-8's eyes were big from the shock she received from Norcotic making her deep throat, and tears started falling from her eyes. Norcotic pulled his dick on out her embrace slowly, but she was sucking so hard that she literally was pulling it back in her mouth with her lips using no hands.

Sluuuurrrrrp, POP!

Tra-8 sucked on his pole throwing her head fast, twisting it, and rolling her tongue as she went, causing Norcotic to bust a nut all inside her mouth. It was so much sperm filling her cheeks that it started oozing out of her nose.

"Swallow it, baby!" he said.

Tra-8 loved the taste of Norcotic's salty sperm dripping down her throat. She especially loved the way it shot in her mouth, busting all over her lips, making her mouth feel like it was full of hot, thick syrup.

Tra-8 did as she was told, pulling away from Norcotic and looking in his eyes as she sucked on her fingers telling him, "Your dick is delicious! Now let me suck on them phat ass balls while you massage my pussy, daddy."

Norcotic let Tra-8 suck on his walnuts while he played with her clit until she busted a nut of her own.

"Ummm, I want you to bust into this pussy so bad, nigga. Come dog this pussy. Please Norcotic, dog the shit out this pussy, you sexy motherfucker."

Norcotic was looking at Tra-8's pussy lips spilling liquid

fire from out of her pussy hole, and he wanted to feel that wet ass pussy so bad. Norcotic grabbed the remote to Tra-8's CD player and pressed play. Beyoncé's song, "That's How You Like It" with Jay-Z filled her room, and Norcotic put the song on repeat. When the first verse started, Tra-8 started singing along while she rolled her hips lying on her back.

"I need a thug that's gonna have my back Du-rag, Nike airs to match Ain't nothing wrong with that."

Norcotic took off his shirt and swagged to the beat getting a laugh from his girl. Hearing her sexy laugh made him dance a little harder.

"Oh, so you like that, Norcotic?" "I like it if you love it, baby."

Tra-8 was staring at Norcotic seductively which made him make a face like a monster and growled like a savage pit bull. DMX could not have done it any better. He stood over Tra-8's head, reached down, and grabbed her by the hips, flipping her upside down so her soaking wet pussy was right where it needed to be. Pushing her upside-down body against the wall, Norcotic snacked on her pussy like a death row inmate eating his last meal.

"Oh shit! You big eared motherfucker! Eat this pussy boy, got DAMN!" Tra-8 was cumming all over Norcotic's face. "Tell mommy how good that pussy taste, mommy taste good don't it? You sexy motherfucker. EAT THIS PUSSY!"

Norcotic could taste her juice flowing and his mouth was filling with so much pussy juice that his cheeks looked like *Ed, Edd, n Eddy* hiding jawbreakers in their cheeks. Norcotic spit cum back all on her pussy using one hand to keep her on the wall and the other to slap her ass. He started eating her pussy again making her cum eight more times. By this time, Norcotic's face looked like he rubbed his head in baby oil. Tra-8 saw his face and laughed while she stroked his beard.

"Oh my god look at you. I'm sorry, hahaha," she laughed with a big smile on her face. She was having a good time and that made Norcotic happy.

"At least your beard is really soft," she joked.

"Oh, you think this shit is funny, honey?" he asked her.

"A little bit."

"We'll see how funny it is when I'm fucking the shit out of your sexy ass all over this room," he teased.

"Oh no, I'm scared," Tra-8 mocked her man, giving him motivation to beat her pussy up.

Norcotic picked Tra-8 up and threw her on the bed where she got in doggy-style position twerking while slapping her ass and looking back at Norcotic. He couldn't stop himself from sliding his tongue down the crack of her ass letting her dance to the pleasure.

"Ummm, eat that ass, nigga!" Tra-8 said, shaking her ass on Norcotic's face while he tried to suck a fart out of her sexy ass. When Norcotic got up for some fresh air, Tra-8 put her face in a pillow, gripped both her ass cheeks, and spread them as far apart as she could.

This action needed no introduction, and nothing could explain the feeling when Norcotic pushed his penis into her soft puddle of water making his whole dick super wet. Norcotic bounced on her succulent ass cheeks while using his thumb to explore her anus. Tra-8 was still talking shit.

"Do it harder baby, come on, Fuck me! I missed you so much and I am always a good girl. Now punish this pussy something terrible. Just fucking do me dirty, please baby," she moaned, and Norcotic turned up.

SMACK! SMACK! SMACK! SMACK!

Norcotic was nailing her pussy so forcibly and powerfully that her head was putting cracks in the headboard.

"Ouch, nigga, you hurting me!" she screamed.

"Bitch, shut the fuck up and take this dick!" Norcotic yelled, gripping her hips so tight that he felt his fingers on the other side.

He had his thumbs in the dimples on the small of her back and he was in and out of the pussy so fast, that Flash would have been jealous. Pulling his dick out of her swollen pussy after she nutted all over his balls, Norcotic threw his football dick in the end zone of her booty making her limp body go rigid from the pain.

POP!

That was the sound of her booty being busted open, and Tra-8 screamed bloody murder.

"Noooooo! Daddy, not in my ass, no! Please take it out, take it out please. I was just talking shit," she cried, trying to reach back and pull his dick out herself.

Slapping her ass and fucking her like a cave man, Norcotic started talking shit back to her.

"Yeah bitch, look at yo soft ass, talk that dumb shit now, you pretty, phat pussy bitch. I love this good ass pussy. Had you sucking on my dick and slurping my shit, I'll fuck you up in this bitch. Keep playing with me with yo soft ass booty. Damn I wanna melt in that ass."

"Yes, hurry up and melt in my ass, baby, milk that phat ass nut all in my ass!" Tra-8 threw her ass back and Norcotic hit it harder.

"You gon' get up and go cook for me after I stretch this booty out?" he asked her.

"Yes, Norcotic, just hurry up because you tearing my ass

up, nigga, damn!" Tra-8 replied.

She was looking back at him with tears in her eyes and at that moment Norcotic busted a cool nut deep inside them fire ass cheeks that put the furnace out inside of her booty forever. Tra-8 fell on her stomach feeling Norcotic trying to pull out of her grip.

"No baby, stay up inside of me, don't move, just stay in me."

"Okay Tra-8," Norcotic laid in the bed with Tra-8.

"I love you, nigga, 381 forever," she said before they both fell asleep.

Norcotic woke up in Tra-8's room to the smell of eggs and bacon, and instantly his stomach did a Nick Cannon *Drumline* drum roll. Getting up from the bed, Norcotic found his clothes on the floor, and put them back on to go find Tra-8. Pulling the closet doors open, Norcotic pulled out a safe and stashed all the money from the duffle bag except for $20,000 inside. Putting everything back where he got it, he walked upstairs and was greeted by Tra-8 and her cousin, Day-Day. They were already enjoying a meal so as he sat down to join them, Tra-8 got up and fixed her man a plate. Placing it down in front of him, and kissing him on the cheek, Tra-8 asked, "Is that enough for you?"

Norcotic shook his head and wiped the spot she kissed in disgust earning him a playful push.

Day-Day kicked Norcotic under the table and when Tra-8 wasn't looking, he mouthed, "Did you do what I think you did?"

"Hell yeah" Norcotic loudly responded.

"Hell yeah what?" Tra-8 asked looking at Norcotic in a weird manner.

"This food is good, baby. That's all," he replied.

"Oh!" Tra-8 said finishing her meal and taking her plate to the dishwasher.

Norcotic knew Day-Day was talking about the Mansion robbery because he was supposed to go. But when he found out the members of M.A.F.A.R. were going, he backed out. After breakfast, Tra-8 announced she was going to take a nap, but before doing so, she made Norcotic take a shower.

Once out of the shower, Norcotic changed his clothes. He put on a black Sox fitted hat, a short sleeve black, grey, and white button up collar shirt, a pair of black shorts to match his shirt under the button up, and white ankle socks, and a fresh pair of Air Force Ones that had a black Nike check. Before leaving Tra-8's room, he left $20,000 inside her purse. On his was out into the streets, leaving thoughts of that pussy behind, money and world domination took over Norcotic's mind. Day-Day was shooting basketball in the driveway as Norcotic was leaving. Stopping what they were both doing to conversate, the two men greeted with a gentlemen's handshake.

"I'm glad you got up out of there in one piece," Day-Day admitted to Norcotic.

"Yeah bruh, that shit was wild! Ya heard me, shawdy mane? We really could have used you though, but ain't no love lost," Norcotic replied.

Norcotic gave Day-Day a look of hurt trying to emphasize how bad he wanted him on the job. Day-Day squinted his eyes to keep the sweat out and made his facial expression match his feelings. Day-Day did not like Norcotic's friends. He felt that M.A.F.A.R. would eventually turn on him because the vibes he got from them were negative.

"I told you, son!" Day-Day said in his Brooklyn growl, "I got love for you, I really do, but I don't fuck with yo M.A.F.A.R. niggas. It's just something about them, especially that Ice dude," Day-Day said, shaking his head.

Norcotic always respected Day-Day's honesty but that comment reminded him of how Ice never liked the fact that Norcotic started hanging with Day-Day more than M.A.F.A.R.. The first time Norcotic introduced the two men, he was sure there was going to be trouble that day.

"I heard that!" Norcotic agreed only to change the subject, "So what's up! You trying to smoke this Purple Haze with me or what?"

No more words were needed for the companions to send purple clouds to the sky that would get the Gods high. Norcotic and Day-Day grinded the bud and rolled two blunts unaware that there was a third-party ear hustling in on their conversation. This new addition to the party knew he could use the information he'd just heard later. Rusty never did like Norcotic for the simple reason that his thuggish ways are what he wanted his sister and his niece to stay away from. Somehow, he failed at his mission to give his sister's daughter a better life, and that pained him deeply even though he never showed it.

As the vow he gave his sister at her funeral in the Crown Heights section of Brooklyn crossed his mind, Rusty vented, "I'm going to kill that motherfucker if it's the last thing I do."

Norcotic and Day-Day were sitting in the backyard of Rusty's mansion, blowing high-grade weed getting high as a bitch! Now they were on the last one. With nothing going on but the thoughts in their minds, Norcotic noticed a CD player under a table stationed by some folding lawn chairs they were sitting in.

"Is there a CD in there?" Norcotic asked Day-Day.

"I don't know, nigga! Do I look like a motherfucking fairy godmother or something?" Day-Day's response had the two men laughing hard as hell, feeling the effect from the good trees.

Norcotic turned on the CD played and out came the instrumental to a DMX song called the "Ruff Ryders Anthem".

"Oh shit!" Norcotic said, nodding his head to the beat.

"Yeah that X shit be on point, son!" Day-Day said, bobbing his head to the beat too.

Norcotic secretly started to get mad; reaching his boiling point, he snapped.

"Yeah that nigga good, but I'm better, check this shit out?"

Norcotic started freestyling to the instrumental like a seasoned vet.

"My niggas is corrupt, rob yo safe, you bankrupt/ And yo music is like Supahead, your mixtape sucks/ Yeah I got it out the mud, wasn't shit about it luck/

Coming in my hood creeping, lift yo heaters, hit 'em up/ Blow a fuse cuz you cartoons is sitting Donald Ducks/ That's an easy target, spark it, niggaz getting plucked/ Talking 'bout you go hard, shawdy I don't give a fuck/

You ain't gotta push me to the edge, bitch I'm bout to jump/

Bust yo bitch pussy open in her Red Bottom pumps/ Mane yo girl like a squirrel got her mouth full of nuts/ And my pockets got cheese like a pizza's stuffed crust/ Putting Band-Aids on the ice cuz the jewels cut/

New York thug chick never liked the Knicks/

That why I fucks with her cuz she stay copping bricks/
Southside Richmond, we pitching for the doe/
Told her I can make it rain deer, Rudolf the red nose/
Got more O's than bowls full of Cheerios/
Hit the block and I breakfast like cereal/
Dope in they veins, whole hood moving train/ Projects
work for Amtrak, catch drains, Ajax/
Dump sacks, was the middleman, now I front packs/ Run
up in the Mansion, like Doug Wilber, where it's at?/ 24 bars
ain't nothing for me/
Turning tricks in the game like, fuck you, pay me/
For a whole 30 seconds, Day-Day just stared at Norcotic in
complete silence. Then out of nowhere he screamed at the top
of his lungs, causing birds in the nearby trees to fly away
startled from the loud noise created by the thrilled human.

"What the fuck, son! You never told me you could spit!"
Day-Day yelled, looking at Norcotic like he just broke a world
record for something, but all Day-Day could think about was
the potential millions he could make pushing Norcotic's
music.

"Yeah, my nigga, I've been spitting raps since I was ten
years old. Shit even before then, but I started going to the
studio with my mentor, Big Sty, for a couple of months now,
but we ain't really doing nothing with it," Norcotic replied.

Norcotic thought about his true passion and how he
would love to leave the streets alone and chase his dreams, but
for now, that was not an option.

"That sounded like some up-top shit with a down south
voice!" Day-Day said still impressed with Norcotic's lyrical
skills.

Norcotic never saw his friend like this. Usually Day-Day

would be very cool, calm, and collected, but after hearing Norcotic's freestyle, he was extremely excited.

"I'm not trying to get on or nothing like that, I just do this shit for the love of music. Rappers don't really perfect the craft of the 16 bars like they used to. Plus, I got to show them New York niggas that us Virginia boys can really spit," Norcotic explained, but Day-Day had different plans for his friend.

"Look, fuck all that bullshit, son. Come on, we gotta go find my pops!" Day-Day didn't even wait for Norcotic to respond or agree before grabbing his arm and pulling him to his feet and towards the house.

Rusty had been watching the whole exchange between his son and his niece's boyfriend, so when the men rushed the house, Rusty hung up the phone he was on leaving a message that would put an end to Norcotic's life. He instantly picked up a magazine as if he were reading and minding his business. Rusty picked the magazine up so quickly that he never noticed he had the magazine upside down. Rusty being the powerful man he was, had called some of his most trusted associates to hire a hitman. Rusty had heard about Norcotic through the grapevine and the one thing everybody agreed on about the young man was that he was a true western with a pistol. Also, for his age, he was as dangerous as they come. Not one to underestimate anyone, Rusty got his powerful friends to lead him in the direction of the greatest hitman ever.

His research and resources had made him aware of a man by the name of Shydow. Some people just called him Shy, not because it was the first three letters of his name, but for the fact that no one has ever seen him in person. Well, except for his victims, who never lived to reveal the identity of their hitman. Shydow earned that name respectively because he was like a true shadow. Furthermore, it was said that not one person had ever heard his real voice. That was confirmed when Rusty called the hitman and was answered by a monstrous voice explaining to leave a name, phone number and a price.

"G, 8044-292-4537, and the price is $100,000."

Rusty was able to hang up the phone and pick up the magazine, pretending to read before his living room door came flying open with the force of a trap house door being kicked off the hinges by the narcs. Day-Day followed by Norcotic came rushing into the living room like a stampede out of the African jungle. The first thing Norcotic noticed was that a nervous acting Rusty was sitting in a La-Z-Boy chair, reading a magazine upside down. Rusty looked up to see what was going on.

"Fuck you little niggas doing busting through my door without knocking?" he asked them.

"Pops!" Day-Day said waving at Norcotic, "This nigga can spit!"

Norcotic was standing there looking at Day-Day as if his mind had traveled through the Bermuda Triangle, because it was obvious that he had lost it. Rusty was happy and sad at once because he had not seen his son this happy since back in Brooklyn, before he had done federal prison time. This was before Day-Day grew up to resent his father because he was never there. As father and son, their relationship was constantly going up and down. Rusty saw this as an opportunity to make Day-Day happy. On the other hand, the man he was ready to have killed was the reason for his son's excitement.

But oh well, sometimes people had to go for more opportunities to grow.

Thinking of how he could kill two birds with one stone, the light bulb shined the brightest idea into his dusty brain. He could sign Norcotic to his record label, help him blow up on his G-Fam Record label imprint, and when Shydow killed Norcotic, the label would get the publicity it needed to assist his artist Dee-I in becoming a superstar. Nobody would ever think that Rusty had anything to do with Norcotic's death, sort of like the situation with Suge Knight and Tupac, or Puff Daddy and Biggie Smalls. The most important outcome of the plot was that Rusty could please Day-Day in the process, while ridding Tra-8 of a no good boyfriend. When Norcotic died, the pieces of the puzzle could be put back together by the person who scattered them in the first place, and he'd look like the good guy.

"So. What's that got to do with me?" Rusty played along, as if he wasn't going to help the boys.

"What the fuck you mean what's it got to do with you?" Day-Day screamed getting mad, "Because you got a record label. Just hear the nigga out, Pops! He can really rap and he's better than that Dee-I dude." All the pieces to the puzzle were falling like Rusty needed with Day- Day's rant.

"Okay! I'll hook you up with my DJ, Sinister Shan." Rusty replied.

Norcotic had listened to all Sinister Shan's mixtapes and dreamed for a long time of working with the Firemen DJs, Sinister Shan and DJ Greg Nasty. They were the best production team in the underground circuit, and highly respected in the music industry.

"Thanks, Rusty!" Norcotic expressed his gratitude and appreciation to deaf ears, to have Rusty cut him off slicker than greased scissors.

"Yeah, yeah, now get out of my house. I got work to do." Rusty pushed Day-Day and Norcotic towards the exit then slammed the door behind them.

"Mane, I can't believe your Pops knows Sinister Shan. That's crazy!" Norcotic exclaimed.

"Yeah yo, that nigga know people, but look, we gonna go check Sinister Shan at the studio tomorrow. Go get that CD out of the player in the backyard and get with me in the morning. I'm about to go get a shower and go handle some business," Day-Day told Norcotic.

"No doubt!" Norcotic said, heading towards the back of the mansion to get the instrumental with thoughts of his rap dreams on his mind.

On his way from retrieving the CD from the backyard, Norcotic bumped into Tra-8. She was rested, and dressed in knee-length Red Bottoms, a black leather pencil skirt, and a red, silk, collared shirt tied in a butterfly knot in the front. She had gold doorknockers hanging from her ears, and she was glowing in the sun looking absolutely wonderful.

"Hey baby, where are you going?" Norcotic eyed Tra-8 suspiciously, as she stood with her hands on her hips with a New York attitude, clutching a red Hermes Birkin bag that matched her outfit.

"Boy! With all that money you left in my bag, I'm going shopping!" Tra-8 laughed and asked, "What about you Mr. Ask My Girl Her Whereabouts; what are you about to do?"

"I got some running around to do, but look, we got to talk later, so I'ma get at that ass later. Okay?" Norcotic said.

Tra-8 looked at Norcotic in a way as to say did he think she was stupid.

"Norcotic, you've been gone for some shit! So, you had

better make sure yo ass is back here. Trying to give me some hush money and shit, nigga. Please bring your ass back! Or if you ain't coming back, just answer your damn phone," Tra-8 said, slapping Norcotic on the arm.

Norcotic slapped her back but on her butt, which got her moving in the direction of her Jeep Cherokee.

"I hope you do get at this ass!" Tra-8 said, shaking her tail a little as she climbed into her jeep.

Things were looking good for once, but little did Norcotic know, things were about to get really bad!

CHAPTER 3

III

"Da Quiet Before The Storm"

In a secluded area in the middle of Chesterfield County was a man training in a room that was truly hell on earth. To say the room was sponsored by the devil himself, was an understatement. There were four soundproof walls that enclosed a cement floor, big enough to put a football field inside. There were no windows in the structure to peep out into the world around him. That was done purposely. It would keep the man focused. In the middle of the room was a boxing ring and on the other end was a gun range. Weapons of all varieties were neatly stacked on a table, and there were weights for exercising in different sizes and shapes to help enhance one's power.

It was already midnight and the man they called Shydow had been training for three hours staring at pictures of all his past victims in their death state. His workout regimen for the day consisted of an hour of yoga, 1,000 push-ups, 1,000 sit-ups, 500 pull-ups, a 5-mile run, and 30 minutes of shadow boxing at full speed in the boxing ring. For all the working out that Shydow did, he was not a big man at all, just cut up and in tip-top shape. Standing at 5'9 and weighing only 190 pounds of pure muscle, one had to be an animal to even think of contesting the monster that was trapped inside of this man. There was still 30 minutes of karate, 30 minutes of shooting, and an hour swim in the indoor pool before he would get any rest.

In between the first and second parts of his regimen, and while making a blended drink with all different kinds of fruit including strawberries, grapes, pineapples, and mango, Shydow decided to check his messages. Turning on his untraceable phone, he noticed that he had 20 missed calls, 10 unanswered texts, and a private message from his second number that gets forwarded to this phone. That second number, only given to serious business partners, was for his job. A job he liked to refer to as Shydow's Cleaning Services. After viewing the information on his phone, he erased the call log and the text history, opting to find out more about who was calling the second number.

"Message box. You have one new message. To hear the recorded message press 1." Shydow pressed 1 and heard a voice that sounded awfully familiar. "G, 804- 292-4537, and the price is $100,000."

Shydow wasted no time calling back the number from the message. Dollar signs were running through his mind. He had never been paid this much money for a hit before. The money pushed the motivation of finishing his workout clean out of his mind as he responded to the caller. The man who he assumed left the message had answered the phone but being a professional, Shydow asked for the person of interest.

"May I speak with G?" Shydow asked through his

automated voice changer, which made him sound like a demon robot.

"This is he." The person responded, knowing he was talking to the hitman himself.

In no laughing manner, Shydow threw 21 questions at G faster than a Major League pitch that Sammy Sosa couldn't have hit in his prime.

"$50,000 up front to be deposited in my offshore account, and the other $50,000 when the job is complete."

Shydow spoke with the confidence of a businessman who was conducting a meeting for an oil tycoon. "Dead or alive?" Was the question, and the answer came back just as serious as the question was given.

"Dead!"

Shydow thought for a minute before continuing,

"And what is the subject's name? I will also need you to send pictures of the target to my email account, along with any valuable information that will help me complete the cleaning."

"Well his name is Norcotic!" Rusty answered after writing down the email and bank account information.

Shydow paused for another minute, not believing that he actually knew who his subject was personally. One thing about money was that it made business, business, and never personal so even though Shydow knew the target and admired the man's heart, that would not stop his death.

"Once the fifty grand is in my account, the storm will take place, and blood will rain down upon the city of Richmond."

Ciera was in complete dismay over her parents' deaths, but this was no time to mourn. There would be plenty of time for that at the funeral; now was the time for revenge. Blu jumped in her Mazda Z and slammed on the gas pedal so hard she could have surely gotten a ticket. Blu was in a daze as she drove. She arrived at her destination so fast, if it were not for the change of scenery, she would have thought that she never left the house. *How could someone storm pass security and kill multiple people, then disappear like some kind of magic trick?* Blu though as she was driving her car, getting closer to her destination. Pulling up and parking her car in the driveway of one of Richmond's most expensive homes, Blu got out and prepared to ring the doorbell. She was mentally prepping herself for the argument she was sure to receive for her visit. She did not call the occupant of this home and it was now well after midnight, but her sanity was at stake, making her determination level extremely high. Blu regained her confidence and rang the doorbell of the head director's house. Not receiving an answer for nearly 15 minutes, Blue repeatedly pressed the doorbell until the foyer lights were turned on, and the locks were being unlocked on the door.

Chauncey answered the door cautiously, but very irritated holding a service gun in his hand. Standing in his boxer shorts, a white T-shirt and a robe, he squinted through his glasses at his visitor and shook his head in disapproval.

"What the hell, Ciera! It's almost one in the morning."

Blu did not wait to be invited in, but instead walked right into the director's home, and straight to the mini bar she had become familiar with from all the past Christmas parties.

"Well, why don't you just come on in, Ciera, make yourself at home," Chauncey whispered to himself before closing his front door.

Chauncey knew that Ciera's parents were murdered very

viciously, and that she needed support from family and friends, but to his surprise, she was not emotional or sad, but very pumped up and angry. Blu grabbed a bottle of Bacardi 151 and a shot glass.

"You want a drink, director?" Blu asked Chauncey as if it were her house, and she was entertaining a houseguest.

"Sure, why not!" Director Chauncey said, putting his gun in the drawer of an end table and closing it shut.

Blu poured a shot, handed it to the director and started drinking straight from the bottle like it was water and she'd just finished running a mile in the Sahara. Blu sat down and burped loudly.

"So ladylike," Chauncey replied to the rudeness.

"Excuse me," Blu said with a sad frown gracing her pretty face, which nearly broke the director's heart in half.

Who knew what to say to someone who lost their parents in such a hideous homicide? Chauncey let the silence do the talking. Feeling the stillness was not appropriate for the moment, he decided to offer his condolences.

"Blu, I'm sorry about…"

"Just shut up!" Blu said, jumping to her feet in a drunken posture pointing a finger at the director's chest, "And you, you put me back on my parents' case!"

Chauncey grabbed her hand to keep her from falling, as she was swaying back and forth, but the fire in her eyes was that of a determined woman on a mission.

"Now, Blu, you know I can't put you on this type of case. Your emotions could get the best of you, and instead of arresting suspects, you may use your power as an agent to have them eliminated. I'm sorry but I just can't let you on the case, Blu," Chauncey explained.

Blu started to cry onto the director's chest while he stroked her hair like a protective father comforting his child. After a while of soaking the director's shirt with tears filled with salty sadness, Blu started taking off her clothes.

"Blu, what the hell are you doing?" he asked.

"Until you put me on the case, I'm going to piss and shit all over your expensive ass furniture," Blu said before squatting down and straining until her face turned red.

"NOOO!" Director Chauncey screamed. "Ok, Ok, Okay! You are back on the case, Blu, but whatever you do, please do not take a shit on my Polar Bear rug. I got that from the Artic and it's very expensive. For the love of me don't shit on my rug!"

Blu stood up and jumped on the sofa yelling "Thank You!" repeatedly. The combination of liquor and the motion of Blu jumping up and down caused Blu to throw up all over the place. Director Chauncey just shook his head and walked away to his bedroom, slamming the door behind him.

"Sorry, Director Chauncey!" Blu said to an empty room.

Blu was so excited that she lay down on the sofa, not even cleaning up her mess. She fell asleep, naked, lying in her spew, as she dreamed of catching her parents' killers.

CHAPTER 4

III

"Love and War"

The day before, Tra-8 went to the mall to go shopping with her girl, Byrd. Tra-8 and Byrd had a long history together, but through the good, the bad, and the ugly, the girls never separated like most girls do, they only became better friends. Norcotic had given Tra-8 $20,000, so she decided to pick her girlfriend up for a day out on the town and catching up. Tra-8 gave Byrd $5,000 to shop with her so she wouldn't be the only one spending money, and the girls balled throughout the mall like a couple of ball player's wives. Tra-8 bought Prada heels and sunglasses along with two Prada skirts. Byrd bought a PlayStation game console and a few games, saying she was going to save the rest for a rainy day. Byrd wasn't broke by a longshot, but Tra-8 always looked out because her own situation was more than fabulous.

Tra-8 wanted to do something special for Norcotic to let him know she was thinking about him, and that she appreciated the money he had given her, so she made plans to buy him something.

"Aye Byrd, do you know anyone who could sell me a pound of some good ass weed, and a gun? Something like an AK-47?" Tra-8 asked.

"Girl! What the heck are you going to do with a pound of weed and an AK-47?" Byrd wanted to know with concern written all over her face; Tra-8 laughed.

"It's not for me, silly. It's for Norcotic. I want to buy him something and I don't really know what to get him," Tra-8 responded.

"Why don't you buy him some Jordan's, a couple of hats or a game or something, why do you want to buy him a pack?" Byrd asked.

"Because I want to show him his baby can be a little gangsta too!"

Byrd just shook her head at Tra-8 but was relieved that the product and chopper was not for her.

"Oh, okay, I can put Norcotic on to some real shit, it ain't nothing." As they walked into a sneaker store known as The Downtown Locker Room, or DTLR, Tra-8 and Byrd became the center of attention. They caught the eyes of everyone in the store; all the other shoppers were looking at the girls with either jealousy or lust.

"Dammmmnnnn nigga, take a picture!" Byrd said to one of the people who was grilling her like a piece of steak.

Byrd had on a pair of blue Seven jeans, some all-white Jordan 5s, and a tight-fitting Polo shirt. Her curves were to die for, and people were literally dying to get a taste of her flavor.

"I know that's right!" Tra-8 followed up before heading over to the wall of shoes.

While looking at a pair of pink and white Reebok pumps. Tra-8 could not help but notice a person eyeing her lustfully.

She couldn't lie, the guy was very, very attractive. He was tall like a ball player, light skinned, and donning a tank top showing off the many tattoos that covered his muscular frame. It was obvious that he worked out, and Tra-8 found herself thinking, "I wonder what gym this fine ass nigga be working out at?" His waves were spinning viciously, and he had a smile that could warm the coldest of nights. Tra-8 couldn't help but smile back; but feeling embarrassed, she looked away.

"You know that dude or something, Tra-8?" Byrd asked.

"Nah!" she replied to Byrd who looked like she wasn't buying that.

"I see y'all two smiling at each other and shit. So, either y'all know each other or somethings going on, and you ain't giving me no details, bitch!" Byrd said, playfully pushing Tra-8 as they talked.

"Girl, I don't know that nigga, but he could get it though," Tra-8 said.

"If I was you, I'd give it to him," Byrd said noticing the guy still eyeing them like a hawk in the sky.

"Boo, I got a man at home, OK! I don't need a pretty boy when I got a handsome man at home," Tra-8 reasoned aloud, while entertaining the thought of cheating on Norcotic.

Earlier that day, it had crossed her mind that Norcotic had been gone for three days with his phone off, yet he never mentioned where he was. She didn't think to ask because she was just happy to see him, and she hadn't wanted to ruin the mood with an argument over unanswered calls and texts. He never apologized for his absence. He never introduced her to any of his friends and he was always in the streets. She thought about how he treated her family, Day-Day, like a brother, and bought nice things for her. However, he didn't have a job, which made her question where and exactly how he got his money?

"He's coming over here," Byrd whispered, bringing Tra-8 out of her thoughts.

When Tra-8 looked up she saw him walking over towards them and she started to get edgy.

"Girl, I'm going to be over here," Byrd said, pointing her thumb away from where Tra-8 was standing. "At least see what the nigga is about, shoot! He might got some money," Byrd said, walking away now, leaving her friend to fend off the boy by herself.

The guy walked over with pure arrogance.

"Why did your friend just leave you like that, all alone, by yourself? I don't understand, cause if I were your friend, I would never leave your sexy ass alone," he asked; Tra-8 smiled. He took that as an invitation to continue, "If your name is as beautiful as your smile and any reflection of the woman you are, then you ain't nothing but trouble, Miss Lady."

"Well if I'm trouble you better be careful before you find yourself in it," Tra-8 said with much attitude hoping her aggressive body language would scare away the guy's advantages, but it seemed to only make him try harder.

"If this is what trouble looks like, I can see why half the world starts it, only to be in you." His response made Tra-8 wet between the legs, and she giggled nervously.

"What's so funny, cutie? Because I'm dead ass serious. I haven't laughed in a while, so I could use a good joke to lighten the mood because your swag got my heart anticipating a rejection," he continued.

The guy then offered his name, and Tra-8 gave hers in return. She became intrigued and very interested in the stranger the more they talked, and they ended up exchanging numbers before they left the store. They never purchased anything, it was as if the store's only purpose was for them to meet, not buy sneakers.

The next day came like an orgasm from heaven, bringing unexplainable pleasure to Tra-8. Today, she had Rusty's mansion to herself, and the events of yesterday were like four play leading up to the backed up nut of the present moment. The doorbell rung sounds of wind chimes throughout the mansion, and Tra-8 ran like a schoolgirl to open the door. She quickly opened the front door to be greeted by the guy she met at the mall yesterday.

"What's up, Ice; come in."

Rusty, Day-Day, and Norcotic were riding in Rusty's black Mercedes CLS550 Benz headed towards the G-Fam recording studio located on the city's East end on Fairmount and 22nd Street. All Norcotic was thinking about was using this opportunity to impress Sinister Shan. Rusty was on his cell phone telling someone to open the door. Within seconds, they were pulling up to the curb of a big, blue building. Rusty told Day-Day and Norcotic to get out of his car, and as soon as the two men stepped out, Rusty sped off. A big metal door opened on the building, which looked abandoned from the outside. The man who opened the door looked like a black version of Bain from the *Batman* movie. He was 6'7 and built like an athlete.

"Let's go!" he said to Day-Day and Norcotic, leading them pass the big, metal door.

Securing the door behind them, he spoke in a deep voice

telling them to go forward. They all walked down a long hallway and came to an elevator at the end. It opened up for them as soon as they arrived. Once on, the elevator's doors closed and in about ten seconds they stopped. The elevator doors opened again, and what Norcotic saw blew his mind away. There were a dozen females, sexier than you average models, dressed in cat suits that were decorated to the G-Fam logo. Everybody in the room was drinking expensive wine and smoking good weed. The room must have been soundproofed because the music was blaring at a deafening level but on the elevator, nothing could be heard.

Norcotic searched the room with his eyes, scanning his surroundings. This was like a dream come true for the young hustler. The studio housed the greatest speakers that money could buy. There was a Triton keyboard and a MPC3000 Beat Machine in the corner. Flat screen monitors were all over the room, and various musical instruments were scattered all over the place. The G-Fam logo had been stenciled, and imprinted on almost everything, including the leather sofas and chairs. There was even a huge mixing board next to a banging set of turntables, and a soundproof glass window, which displayed the recording booth on the other side.

Sitting in front of the mixing board was Sinister Shan himself, in the flesh! Sinister Shan was the music game's biggest producer, and he had produced for some of the biggest stars. That included Lil Wayne, Juelz Santana, Swizz Beats, Jay-Z, and Eminem. Sinister Shan was half- white and half-Italian, but he was born and raised in the Bronx. He was an average height and slender, but Norcotic noticed the big pistol on his hip instantly.

As Day-Day, Norcotic, and their escort stepped into the

studio, they caught the attention of Sinister Shan. He stopped the music, lit a blunt, and waved them over.

"Yo kid! You ready?" he asked.

"I was born ready; ready wasn't ready for me!" Norcotic replied.

Sinister Shan turned around in his swivel chair and pressed a button that turned on one of the hardest beats Norcotic had ever heard in his life. From the sounds of the instrumental, you immediately knew that it was one of Sinister Shan's own beats. All the girls were looking at Norcotic and giggling as they whispered to each other.

"Step in the booth and let's see what you got then!" Sinister Shan told Norcotic.

Once Norcotic was inside the recording booth, he looked through the glass that separated the booth from the control room while he applied the headphones to his ears and adjusted the mic. Day-Day, Sinister Shan, and everybody else in attendance were waiting to see Norcotic perform. While they were all anticipating what he was going to rap on the mic, Dee-I stepped in from the elevator with his entourage. Norcotic had never seen Dee-I in person but recognized him from all the flyers and posters that were all over the city.

"Who's the kid in the booth?" Dee-I asked Sinister Shan.

"I don't know, Rusty called and said he had a new addition to the label and for me to see if he was worth the investment," Sinister Shan replied.

Dee-I hearing this became instantly envious of Norcotic. Dee-I was the label's only artist and had been trying to blow up for a couple of years now with no real luck. With another artist on the label, Dee-I would have to compete for recording time, drop dates, and promotion money.

Everybody was looking at Norcotic through the glass and on cue with life, Norcotic started talking shit through the mic to the beat, "Yeah nigga, yeah! (yeah nigga yeah!), It's coming! (it's coming!), I know you feel that shit (you feel it). You just in your whip right now that shit knocking you. You just nodding your fucking head, yeah, YO!"

Then Norcotic began to spit, no pen, no pad, no written lyrics to read, just straight creative energy from the heart.

"Yo, let's go!

Feeling like the whole world wants me laid in a casket/
They coming for my neck and the head that's attached to it/

Plus, the crown cuz I'm sitting on the throne/

So, I gotta keep the ratchet clapping, spitting at your dome/

They want my position, I'm fresh out the kitchen/ The best up in Richmond them niggaz can't get it/ And no disrespect but I'm next, I can feel it/

So, tell all them rappers that Norcotic in the building/ Been up in the trenches with shells in my pistol/

That's bigger than my middle finger, fuck all you niggaz/

Every victim I had, they know I pull triggers/My team can bust hollow tips or let off a missile/

Never leave a witness, they potential snitches/ Rat, then we'll pull your teeth out like the dentist/ Dee-I in the studio screaming G-Fam/

Signed to the Dope Boys, he about to go ham/

Wit a Big Mac and a Whopper down to get murder/ Mane on a T-shirt the only time we heard of you/ Finally teamed up and glad that we merging/

Killing every rapper and we'll never show 'em mercy/

Chocolate trees, my weed was made by Hershey/

And the smell stronger than that nigga Hercules/ Purple leafs, we be blowing up that good chronic/ Yo Sinister Shan, you're now rocking with Norcotic/

Norcotic was spitting bars of fire in the booth that could've burned down a fire hydrant. The more he rapped, the more the girls danced with the fellas looking on in amazement. Dee-I was beyond shocked, but he didn't want to show it at all. He knew that if Norcotic's music started to get out with him rapping like that, he would not blow up. At that moment, he started plotting a way to get Norcotic out of the picture.

"Yo! Come out," Sinister Shan demanded through Norcotic's headphones.

As Norcotic came out of the booth, Sinister Shan was playing the freestyle over again, and with the adlibs over the beat, the song sounded fucking bananas; it was a hit.

"Yo, kid!" Sinister Shan called to Norcotic in his Bronx lingo, "You nice man, just keep it up." Sinister Shan didn't usually give out compliments because over the course of the years, he'd heard a lot of rappers and nothing really impressed him, but he thought there was something truly special about Norcotic. "I didn't think down south niggas could rap like that!"

Norcotic felt like this was a moment for him to elaborate.

"With me, I know people feel that way about rappers from the south. That's why I spit the way I do, to prove that it doesn't matter where you're from but it's what's in your heart that matters." He finished his statement looking at Dee-I, who was nodding his head in agreement.

"That's real la-homie," Dee-I said before leaving with the models. He was heading to his video shoot that he was already late for.

Sinister Shan told Norcotic to get ready because they were

going to the video shoot also. Norcotic looked at Day-Day who already knew what Norcotic was going to say.

"Nah, son! I can't go. I gotta go home and handle some business. You go have a good time though!" Day-Day said before Norcotic asked anything.

"No doubt!" Norcotic replied to his soul brother.

"Besides, I don't fuck with Dee-I anyway; that's my father's people."

Norcotic knew Day-Day didn't rock with too many people so he just said thank you and prepared to leave with Sinister Shan and Dee-I's entourage.

Tra-8 and Ice wasted no time indulging in recreational festivities to increase the chemistry that was building between the two. They drunk and smoked together to the point they were pissy and high as gas. Once it came to the point that even the slightest blow from the lips could be felt as if the wind blew her melody, Ice began touching Tra-8 in places that sent electricity through her body. They were all over each other passionately caressing and kissing as if their lips could cool the heat. They were dry humping through their clothes so hard that they forgot that actually had clothes on. Tra-8 thought to herself, *I barely even know this nigga!* Truth be told, there were three things about Ice that Tra-8 did not know. Things that if she had known, she would have not even come close to talking to him at DTLR in the first place.

She had no idea that Ice was the general of M.A.F.A.R. MAFIA, a gang of masterminds that she's heard of from all the robberies and killings throughout Virginia that shocked the community. She had no idea that Ice had laced her alcohol with a date rape drug. The shots she took after the blunt they smoked, left her vision blurry and her thoughts unclear. Her tolerance for weed and liquor was fairly high so after the shot she summed up her current fucked up state to experiencing new emotions for someone different. Tra-8 was on the verge of being unconscious. The last thing she was unaware of was the fact that the man who was now taking advantage of her sexually was her boyfriend's best friend.

Soon as Ice spotted Tra-8 in the mall spending hundreds of dollars like she had no care in the world, he started plotting on the caramel beauty. He figured there had to be more money where that came from, and he was right. What Ice did not know was that Tra-8 was Norcotic's girl, Ice had known Norcotic since the two were in elementary school; they were thicker than blood, and one would have thought that a friend would introduce his love to his best friend. However, Norcotic always kept business, family, and the streets totally separated from each other. Ice had no idea he was about to rob Norcotic and rape his girlfriend.

E-Youngin, Sincere, and Legion were all outside in a black, stolen, MPV van waiting for Ice to text them letting the crew know that it was safe to come in.

"Yeah bitch! You like this dick don't you! You good pussy having slut." Ice yelled at Tra-8.

WHAM! WHAM! WHAM! WHAM!

The sounds of Ice's large larceny dick echoed throughout the empty mansion as he bounced on her pussy reminding her of how alone she was. Tra-8 felt herself getting more and more dizzy as the world around her spun full of colors like she was looking through a kaleidoscope. The last thing she remembered before blacking out was Ice laughing, the nut she busted making her feel dirty, and the tears she cried because she betrayed her man. Once Ice saw that the drugs had taken effect all the way, he handcuffed Tra-8 to the bed, and called his team to come in.

He was supposed to text them, but the girl had some of the best pussy the world had to offer. He wanted his boys to hear the excitement in his voice.

"Aye yo, y'all gots to get here quick! This la-baby got a missile between her legs," he said.

"Oh yeah!" Legion replied to his brother, jumping out of the van and running towards the mansion with the other guys in tow.

The men met Ice in the basement and when they saw Tra-8 handcuffed to the bed with her big ass milk chocolate titties spilling out, and her pussy lips dripping wet they went ham!

"Mane, wake this bitch up, she gots to see all of what I'm about to do to that ass!" Legion said rubbing Tra-8's ass with baby oil and Vaseline.

Sincere ran upstairs and found a bucket with a mop in it. He threw the mop aside and filled the bucket with ice and water and went back in the basement. He threw the water on Tra-8 and the freezing water jolted her awake.

"Arrruugghh! What the fuck!" she screamed.

"Bitch, shut the fuck up. Can't nobody hear your trifling ass," E-Youngin said as he slapped the shit out of her.

Tra-8 started bucking against the restraints, trying her best to escape, but the more she fought, the tighter the cuffs became, cutting into her skin.

"Damn!" Sincere licked his lips and said, "If she fucks like how she acting right now trying to get out of them cuffs, then I know that pussy gon be bum as a bitch!"

All the men laughed while preparing to penetrate Tra-8 in every hole.

Legion pulled out his semi-automatic handgun and threatened Tra-8 by slamming the butt of the gun over the top of her head, causing blood to drip from her head.

"Shawty, if you bite my dick one more time, I'ma kill yo stinking ass, now you better suck it right, you hear me, bitch!" he yelled.

"Man chill," Ice schooled his sibling. "What you trying to do, knock the bitch out again?"

Legion's only reply was slamming his dick into Tra-8's mouth.

"Hold on, son!" Sincere said crawling under Tra-8 pushing his dick into her ass while E-Youngin busted her pussy from the top.

There was no remorse for the young lady as the men ripped into her insides like children opening gifts on Christmas morning. They took turns busting nuts into a cup that they planned to make her drink. Somewhere in the hour-long rape, Tra-8 passed out again, only to have Ice wake her up by slapping her ass really hard.

Ice began remixing the Folgers theme song when she opened her eyes back.

"The best part of waking up, is drinking nut out a cup!" The friends all laughed while Ice forced Tra-8 to gulp down the sperm causing her to throw up.

While the boys entertained themselves with their prey, Sincere had ventured off in search of any valuables he could find. He stumbled upon a large combination safe in the closet.

"JACKPOT!" He yelled alerting his team.

They were excited but then they heard the sound of a car door being shut outside.

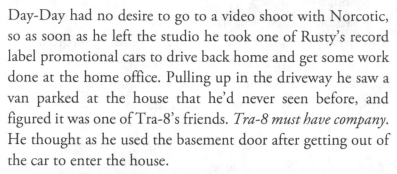

Day-Day had no desire to go to a video shoot with Norcotic, so as soon as he left the studio he took one of Rusty's record label promotional cars to drive back home and get some work done at the home office. Pulling up in the driveway he saw a van parked at the house that he'd never seen before, and figured it was one of Tra-8's friends. *Tra-8 must have company.* He thought as he used the basement door after getting out of the car to enter the house.

"Yo Tra-8!" Day-Day hollered out to no answer.

Day-Day thought it was weird that there was a van outside, but he wasn't getting any responses. Then again, the house was pretty big, so people could have been anywhere. As Ice was pulling the safe out of the closet, Day-Day could be heard yelling Tra-8's name. The men knew there was now an unwanted guest in the house and shit was about to get real.

"Shhhhhh! Stop fucking with that bitch," Ice whispered to Legion who had started pissing on the poor girl.

Footsteps were getting louder and seemed to be closing in on their position. The men took up strategic defenses and attack positions around the room and waited for the new arrival to enter. The door to Tra-8's bedroom opened and in walked Day-Day. Ice couldn't believe his eyes, and Day-Day couldn't believe his. Off instant, he was ready to exit the room. After seeing the familiar faces he thought they were there with Norcotic or Tra-8. On further investigation, Day-Day saw Legion pissing on his cousin and Ice squatted next to a safe. That's when it registered to him that shit wasn't right, and by that time, BOOM!

Sincere punched Day-Day with a full swing that almost separated his head from his neck, but surely fractured his jaw.

Day-Day fell to the floor like a sack of potatoes while the other men stomped on his unconscious body.

"Legion, help me with this safe!" Ice tried getting his brother's attention as he kicked Day-Day viciously.

"That's Norcotic homeboy, right?" Sincere asked the question everybody already knew.

"Mane, fuck that nigga! I hate homeboy anyway.

Norcotic gonna side with us on this one anyway. We M.A.F.A.R.! Now let's go!" Ice roared like a lion at his cubs putting their escape into action.

He had no idea how Norcotic would react to the robbery, but what was done, was already done. If Norcotic wanted smoke though, he would definitely set the fire for him.

Dee-I, Sinister Shan, and Norcotic were at Dee-I's video shoot outside of Rusty's bar and club, The 804 Sports Bar and the G- Spot club. They were smoking the best California Jamaica had to offer and watching the models trying their best to make a name for themselves. Dee-I was a part of a group called the Dope Boys headed by a famous rapper named Spanish Montana. The video shoot was for the hit single "Hit the Pole" by the rapper Boo Town featuring Dee-I. There were expensive cars in the parking lot with foreign names like Murcielago, ContiSportContact 2, Spider, Rolls Royce, and Maybach. The attendance was crazy. Crowds of people were partying in the street like this was a block party, and not even the police could shut the shoot down. While sipping on a bottle of Grey Goose, Norcotic felt a light tap on his shoulders. Turning around he saw someone he hadn't seen in a long time.

"What's up, Norcotic, do you still sleep with a gun under

your pillow?" It was his ex-girlfriend.

"Oh shit! What's up? Give me a hug!" Norcotic said, pulling Byrd into his arms.

Norcotic being caught up in the moment of fun and lust never thought to turn his phone on. He had it turned off to save battery because he did not know how long he would be at the shoot. If he had turned it on, he would've gotten the call to make him flip his top and plot revenger. Since it was off, all he wanted to flip his top was Byrd's sexy lips.

CHAPTER 5

III

"The Set-Up"

After dropping Norcotic and Day-Day off at the studio, Rusty went to collect $50,000 to put into Shydow's bank account. Rusty was a very powerful man in the city of Richmond. He had drug dealers, shooters, and even police and politicians in his back pocket. Rusty truly felt untouchable since, even though he had legal businesses that made him money, most of his income was from selling cocaine. He was the biggest distributor of coke on the East Coast, with his supply coming from the kingpin, Pablo Kane.

Rusty drove in his Benz not even bothering to obey any traffic laws, thinking about plans. In no time, the smooth acceleration and horsepower of the luxury car had Rusty sitting outside his trap house on the Southside of town. Rusty walked into his office and sat behind his desk trying to catch up on some last-minute business before he went to check on his artist at the video shoot. Halfway through the transaction of transferring money to Shydow's account and doing some paperwork for a new building he planned to purchase, Rusty got a nerve wrecking call from a person he least expected to hear from.

"Hello, how are you doing, Blu?"

Day-Day came to his senses after being punched senseless my Sincere's crushing blow. Shaking his head to rid himself of the woozy, dizzy feeling, he stood to his feet and got a feeling of a ship swaying back and forth in a wavy sea. Murder was the only thing on his mind, but the concern for his cousin overrode all emotions. He quickly ran over to her and made sure she was ok. Tra- 8's body was bruised and battered. Standing over her looking down, Day-Day felt a lone tear fall from his eyelids that he wanted to climb back inside. Instead it splashed on her body leaving a small wet dot that symbolized how small he felt for not being able to protect his family.

"Wake up, little momma," Day-Day said. Tra-8 didn't move, even a little, making Day-Day feel the worst he had ever felt in his life. "Tra-8, wake up, cuz," he said while lightly smacking her face.

Tra-8 painfully opened her eyes with fear in her heart, crying the same heart out of her chest, and why not? She would rather be heartless than have one that was tarnished with cruel fingerprints. Day-Day held Tra-8 in his arms and rocked her slowly providing the comfort that only a family member could.

Day-Day had a gift for picking locks, which was why Norcotic wanted him to come on that mission in case there was a safe or locked door they couldn't open. He let Tra-8 go and picked the locks on the handcuffs to free her from the bed. Day-Day picked up the phone and called Norcotic. He couldn't think of why Norcotic's crew would rape his girl unless Norcotic had something to do with it. Either way, Day-Day was going to get to the bottom of this problem and body whoever he found. Day-Day called Norcotic two more times only to get the same results, and the voicemail only pissed him off more.

Throwing the phone with the force of a Major League pitcher. Tra-8 jumped when the phone hit the door, creating a deafening sound in her room and making her cry again.

"It was some guy…." Tra-8 started.

Day-Day stopped her from explaining and let her know he knew exactly who it was that violated. He left the room, charging like a shark after blood heading towards his room. Tra-8 followed slowly, with her body still sore from being raped and beaten. Walking into his room, he threw a bottle of Percs to his cousin that he had on his bookshelf. He occasionally sold them to college students.

Behind the bookshelf was a hidden door to a closet that was big enough to be another room. Inside was a pit-bull named Coco who greeted her master joyfully even though she was a vicious fighting dog. Walking around the closet, Day-Day had Tra-8 help him put on a double panel vest. He then slid two .357s into his waist holster and grabbed two hand grenades. Ready for the mission at hand, he turned to Tra-8 and kissed her on the forehead.

"I got you, Tra-8," he told her.

Norcotic was shocked to see Byrd at the video shoot. His ex was still as beautiful as the day he first met her, if not sexier. She was a 5'8, red-boned with silky black hair that stayed in neat braids. She also had the most intriguing eyes a man has ever seen, and she knew it too. If it weren't for the signature Jordan's, jeans, and button up shirts she constantly wore that gave her a gangsta vibe, she would have been compared to Alicia Keys. With the video shoot being a Southside Superstar kind of event, Byrd traded her Jordan's for wrap around six-inch Prada heels, little jean shorts that revealed an ass shaped like the most delicious forbidden fruit, and a cut up tank top with a knot tied in the back. Byrd had a reputation for being a hood chick that only dated women, but nobody knew that Norcotic had taken her virginity many years ago.

They had remained friends even after they broke up. The two of them still did business with one another with Byrd setting up drug dealers for him to rob. Their dealings with each other caused Tra-8 and Byrd to bump heads leading to a friendship. Norcotic introduced Tra-8 to Byrd on a chance encounter at a local corner store. The women were ready to fight because Tra-8 thought Norcotic was cheating on her. The women eventually became fast friends, and ever since then, Norcotic hadn't seen Byrd, and that was almost over a year ago.

"So, what's up, Byrd? I haven't seen you in a very long time!" Norcotic said, looking Byrd up and down putting a smile on her face.

"Shiiid!" Byrd said, "trying to sell this weed, you know, same old shit."

"Yeah I hear you, shawty." Norcotic replied in his Southern swag.

Byrd started to feel old feelings rushing back. Secretly, she always down played Norcotic like he wasn't nothing, especially in the presence of Tra-8. However, the things she heard about Norcotic in the streets made her pussy melt. She still loved Norcotic with all her heart and started feeling jealous of Tra-8.

She decided to throw salt in the game.

"You know, me and your girl were at the mall the other day, and she was all up in some dude's face and shit."

"Oh, is that right, though?" Norcotic knew she was telling the truth because they had a real, honest relationship with each other. Now he had a vision of Tra-8 taking the money he gave her and buying gifts for another nigga, which he didn't want to show.

"Yeah!" Byrd said flirting with Norcotic hoping that she hit home by revealing Tra-8's disloyalty. "But minus the bullshit, I'm glad I ran into your sexy ass today. Seeing your girl play you like that, kind of made me hate the fact that y'all are still together. I ain't hating or nothing like that. I ain't trying to be your girl or anything but after we left the mall, I got some things for you. I just remembered that you was my only nigga."

"What did you get me?" Norcotic asked, forgetting about Tra-8 talking to another man. In his mind he knew she was loyal to a fault and wasn't going to go anywhere.

"I got you an AK-47 and a pound of Kush," Byrd said, taking credit for the gifts Tra-8 asked for.

"No, you didn't! You ain't get me no AK, shawty, you whaling!" Norcotic said, meaning she was lying, but he was overly worked up.

"Nigga, you calling me a liar like I be snatching on some cheesy shit? Why would I lie to you for? I ain't no clown bitch. It's over at my house right now!" she replied inviting Norcotic to come over and get the gifts.

"Bet, let's go 'cause I got to see this," he said, walking with Byrd to her car.

They drove to her place on the Northside of Richmond.

Day-Day was sitting outside of the M.A.F.A.R. MAFIA trap house saying a prayer. "As I go handle my beef, I pray the Lord my soul to keep, and if I die before my enemies, please let me take half of them with me, Amen!" He finished his prayer by crossing his heart. Walking towards the trap spot, Day-Day cocked his arm back and threw a grenade inside.

Rusty wasn't amazed that Blu had called him. With the murders of Douglas Wilber and Judge Snuckles-Wilber, he knew the FBI would come sticking their noses in his business sooner or later. Rusty had plenty of money, but his specialty was spending it well, and putting paper in the right places to make it work for him. There were many agents in Rusty's pockets, but Blu was not one. She was a hard-working agent and her passion for crime fighting made her impossible to be bought. Law enforcement from every city on the East Coast felt that when something of this magnitude happened, Rusty knew about it or had something to do with it.

Blu knew that Rusty was not the type to play games. Therefore, when he asked how she was doing, even though they were on different sides of the law, she knew he meant every word of concern. This was not the time to be sentimental and vulnerable. Instead of the small talk, Blu went straight to the point.

"My mother and father just died, how in the fuck do you think I'm doing, Rusty? What's funny is, I thought you would have more respect for this situation," Blu said.

"Listen, young lady, you may be a woman of power and I can dig that, but I am a man of respect. No one should have to die like that and I am hurt too. I am hurt for you, but that gives you no right to snap; you called me, remember? Why do you think I asked how you were doing? Because it's not a joke for me," Rusty replied.

"Well for a man that has dirt on his name from the drug game, saying he feels my pain, you sure aren't providing me with lots of information to help me solve this case when you already know what I called for. So, let's do this, I know you heard about something. So, you can either give me a lead, or so help me God, I will use every resource I've got to personally bring you down, and you know I can do it too!" Blu yelled.

Rusty slammed his fist on his desk out of frustration, Blu had him by the balls. If she started an investigation into his operation, either crooked cops or snitches would bring him down. He was already on the FBI's radar, and he had managed to stay afloat in the game this long. Blu was a woman now tormented by the death of her parents and Rusty dared not to play her bluff.

Rusty's came upon a bright idea. He thought about telling her it was Norcotic, because even though he wouldn't wish prison on his worst enemy, it would get the heat off him. With Norcotic on his label now, him being under the eye of the Fed's would continue to give his label the gangsta image it needed.

"Alright, I'll tell you what you need to know. Have you ever heard of Norcotic? He's the guy who pulled that stunt at the Mansion. To be honest with you, his days in the streets are numbered, so all you can do is hope that you get to him first."

Blu knew exactly who Norcotic was, the second leader, and Major of M.A.F.A.R. MAFIA, a gang unit that has been on the FBI's radar for years.

"Are you serious?" Blu said less as a question and more in a way to say she couldn't believe it.

"I'm serious as a heart attack." Rusty was beginning to enjoy the way that he was playing chess with real life pieces and all he could focus on was getting his checkmate.

"Well, how do you know he's in trouble?" Blu asked digging for more information.

"The streets talk, Blu. And Norcotic has managed to piss off some really powerful people on his quest to the top. A contract has been put on his head," Rusty informed her.

This is why Chauncey knew Blu was the perfect agent for the Mansion case. He would have put her on it first thing if it hadn't been her parents that were killed in such a gruesome crime. He knew she could get the water flowing like the Hoover Dam being opened.

"Who's trying to kill the second in charge of M.A.F.A.R. MAFIA, that's like a death wish?" she asked, but the answer gave her an in depth look at how crazy shit was about to get.

"I can't tell you who put the hit out on him, but I can tell you who picked it up!" Rusty said heading out to go to the video shoot, which he was late for.

"Who?" Blu wanted to know who had the balls to kill Norcotic.

"Shydow!" Rusty said before hanging up the phone.

Blu watched her cell phone screen go blank after being hung up on and thought, *The world's most dangerous hitman is now in the mix.*

Rusty made his way to the video shoot. He pulled up and parked his car stepping out of his ride feeling exactly how he looked - Good!

The director was shouting "It's a wrap" to a lot of applause just as Rusty reached Dee-I's trailer finding the man he was looking for.

"Sinister Shan, let me talk to you for a minute," Rusty said not waiting for an answer, but instead taking a seat next to him on the sofa.

"Yo!" Sinister Shan uttered barely audible due to the blunt hanging between his lips.

"Have you seen Norcotic?"

"Yeah, he bounced with some red boned honey in a black car about 30 minutes ago," Sinister Shan replied.

"What do you think about the kid Norcotic; should I put him on the label or not?" Rusty asked.

"The kid can spit! I mean he can really rap. He recorded a freestyle on one of my beats today that was straight fire! He killed it. He doesn't know but I was mixing it while he rapped, and I'm going to put that shit on my next mixtape," Sinister Shan confessed.

Rusty's cell phone rang before the men could finish their conversation. He would have ignored it if it weren't for the ringtone of 50 cents "I Gets Money" letting him know the call was about important business.

"Excuse me for a minute, Shan, I have to take this call."

Rusty answered the phone saying hello as he walked away, and his face went from a look of concern to complete bliss at hearing the information on the other end. His accountant was letting him know the money was successfully transmitted to Shydow's account. The death of Norcotic was now officially in motion.

Ice, Killa, E-Youngin, Sincere, Tiny, Legion, and Mouse were counting the money from their latest robbery. The whole M.A.F.A.R. squad was in tow with the exception of Norcotic who they all figured was with his girlfriend.

"Anybody know where that nigga Norcotic at?" Killa asked the group.

"Naw!" Ice yelled over the Jeezy *Thug Motivation* album that the crew was banging out of the stereo system. "I've been calling him, but his phone is going straight to voicemail. I need to tell him we robbed his boy Day-Day and whoever that bitch was."

"Mane that bitch had some bum ass pussy!" Legion yelled from the other room at the mention of the girl they raped.

"Speaking of mystery bitches and shit, why Norcotic ain't never introduced us to his chick?" Mouse asked. "He always calling her and going to see the girl. You would think if we niggas for real, he'd bring the bitch through to meet us. Norcotic has been on some real funny shit lately like he ain't fucking with us or something. But fuck it, he will come back around when he need us."

Ice didn't know what was wrong with his homey lately, but he was not going to let something petty like if a nigga fucked with him stop the money.

"It's a total of $80,000 in the safe," Sincere announced and then they divided the money into equal shares.

Everybody was given a share of the money, even if they did not take part in the robbery. Ice even put a share to the side for Norcotic, not knowing it was his money to begin with. When he told Norcotic that he robbed his homeboy, Day-Day, he wanted to be able to give him a cut.

"Legion!" Ice shouted at his brother, so he could give him his cut, "Catch!" he said as he threw a stack of money at Legion like a football.

At the same time, a flying object came crashing through

the window and Legion ended up catching that object instead of the money Ice threw at him. When he finally noticed what the object was, it was too late. The look of surprise never left his face when the blast tore his face off and ripped his head from his neck.

KABOOOOOOM!

When the smoke finally started to clear you could make out Day-Day walking into the ravaged calamity that used to be a trap house.

Over on the Northside of town off Chamberlayne Ave. Norcotic and Byrd were inside of her Jackson Ward apartment, which sat on the corner of Hickory and Charity street. As they sat in the living room, busting down a pound of weed to sell by the ounce, they smoked big blunts of Kush and sipped from a bottle of Bacardi 151. The night was young, and while they put the trees in the sandwich bags after being weighed out to 28 grams on a digital scale, they laughed and shared memories of the life they once shared together. Norcotic couldn't believe his eyes when he saw the AK-47. He had never used one before because of their ability to jam. Even though they were the more reliable automatic rifles under the AR-15, but the gun was a beautiful beast and he loved it.

"DAAAAAAAMMMMMMMNNNNN! Thank you again for the heat, shawty. That was some real ass shit, Byrd." Norcotic said.

"It ain't nothing dude, I was just thinking about you, that's all." Byrd made enough money in the streets to get a better apartment than the one she had in the projects, but that was just Byrd. She was gangsta to the core, and never planned on changing. She shot dice, grinded in the hood, and even cooked work up. She was no game when it came to setting niggas up too, that was her M.O. Twisting a knot in the last bag, Byrd stood up.

"Aight, these O's all bagged up. I'm bout to go get my ass in the shower," Byrd said, stumbling towards the stairs taking her clothes off along the way and throwing them all over the room.

Seeing Byrd's phat, juicy ass bounce up and down made Norcotic's dick stand at full attention like a soldier in war. With a mind of its own, his penis did not intend to follow any orders to be at ease. He could not help but remember how good her tight, hairy, diking pussy was. Thinking about the taste of that sweet box between Byrd's legs made Norcotic fall asleep dreaming about fucking the insides out of her pussy hole. He did not know how long it had been since he had fallen asleep when he heard Byrd calling his name from upstairs.

"Norcotic...NORCOTIC!"

"What's up?" he answered back while relighting the blunt he had been smoking before he fell asleep.

"Come wash my back pleeeeeaassee!" Byrd requested.

Norcotic got up out of the chair, walked upstairs, and stepped into the steamy bathroom to a scene right off one of the pages of a Zane book. Scented candles were lit all over the place and Mary J. Blige was singing low from a CD player about a love that had failed but had possibilities of reconciliation. Sparkling water droplets cascaded down her voluptuous body glistening on her frame like lights on a Christmas tree; she was most certainly a gift. The see-through curtain did little to hide her shapely body, instead all it did was pique Norcotic's interest. He walked over to the curtain and slid the cock blocking fabric across the crossbar. Getting a better view of perfection in the form of a woman; she was stunning.

"Here!" she said, handing Norcotic her washcloth and a bottle of Dove body wash. She stared at him seductively as she made her booty clap a little.

Norcotic handed her the blunt he was smoking, making her stand as far away from the shower water so the mist wouldn't ruin the blunt. He washed her back while giving her a firm massage at the same time. A soapy lather slid elegantly down the small of her back between her bubbles for a booty, making Norcotic want to suck a fart out of her plump ass pussy. When he finished, Byrd turned around facing her ex-boyfriend and flicked the roach that used to be a blunt into the toilet. She signaled for him to come closer, and their lips met as if they were introduced for the first time. Byrd expertly blew smoke clouds of Kush into Norcotic's mouth, but it wasn't the smoke that was getting him high.

The blast erupted and ignited total chaos inside the trap house claiming four of the seven M.A.F.A.R. members and leaving the other three critically injured. Day-Day strolled through the smoke and fire looking around for any survivors he could finish off. Travelling over trash and broken furniture, Day-Day came across Legion's severed head and kicked it across the floor like a soccer ball.

"Y'all pussy motherfuckas thought y'all could fuck with me!" Day Day screamed over coughing sounds he heard coming from the living room. Before making his way to the living room, Day-Day turned on the gas stove then followed the sounds of the soon to be departed.

Passing body parts and debris blown about by the impact of the grenades, Day-Day saw nothing but the red in his eyes. Laid by a damaged television, E-Youngin crawled to nowhere fast.

"Don't run now you little bitch!" Day-Day screamed and pressed the barrel of one of his .357 Magnums deep into E-Youngin's eye, shooting a hole clean through his head. His brains had no time to think about living. Not too far from where E-Youngin had been slain, Killa was moaning with his leg broken, and Day-Day decided to cause more pain to the disabled man.

"Arruuggghh!" Killa screamed in pain.

Day-Day was stomping and slamming random objects on Killa's leg. He got bored after a few minutes and blasted four shots in Killa's face with his gun. Under a table, trying to fake like he was dead was Ice. Day-Day saw Ice flinch after he shot Killa in the face, so he knew Ice was still alive. From the looks of it, Ice should not have been his name because the heat from the bomb turned his ass into a puddle.

"What's up, bitch?" Day-Day taunted as he stomped Ice's head. He kicked him in the head so hard half of his teeth came spitting out his mouth. "Look at your pussy ass now, you fucking faggot! Yo bitch ass ain't no gangsta now, are you?" Day-Day said, pulling out the other 357 he had tucked in the holster. Even with half his teeth gone, Ice still tried to talk shit.

"What you say, dog?" Day-Day asked a near dying Ice. "I'm sorry, son, I don't speak fuck nigga! So, you gon' have to translate for me, you bitch ass punk."

Ice motioned for Day-Day to come closer.

"Oh, how sweet of your soft ass, the bitch ass homo thug got some last words. What yo dumb ass got to say, nigga?"

Day-Day kicked Ice directly in the eye forcefully making the eye pop out of his eye socket before bending down to hear what Ice had to say.

"Fuck you, bitch!" Ice whispered spitting blood in Day-Day's face. Day-Day grabbed Ice's eye and pulled it from the cord of flesh that kept his eye attached to his head.

He showed it to Ice.

"I see you want me to fuck you, is that what you said? Well watch this!" Day-Day said, placing Ice's eye on the broken table so that his eye looked as if it were watching what he was about to do. Day-Day pulled Ice's pants down to his ankles and flipped him over like a half-cooked pancake.

He took both Magnums and forcefully stuffed them into Ice's butthole.

"Arruuuugghh!" Ice screamed in excruciating pain.

Day-Day then squeezed both triggers until the guns were empty, sending Ice to a shitty death. Blood and shit were splattered all along the floor from the rapid fire of the 357s. Before leaving, Day-Day soaked the trap house in gasoline and walked out the front door. Still in a religious mood, he spoke to God once more. "God, I had to kill them bitch ass niggas; I had too. At least now hell got a little bit of Ice." Day-Day pulled the pin from his last grenade and threw it into the house.

KABOOOOOOOOM!

Norcotic awoke from a long night's rest still somewhat tipsy off Bacardi 151 shots, to see that he was in a familiar place. It had been years since he went to sleep and woke up in Byrd's house; it was surreal. The last thing he remembered was kissing Byrd in the shower, and the rest was a blank. Rolling over in the bed, removing one of Byrd's legs from his to sit up, Norcotic looked at the clock, lit a blunt, and then turned on the TV to see the local news. The good weed started taking effect and an interesting story caught his attention.

"Hi, I'm Candice Smith reporting to you live where it looks like a drug deal gone bad has claimed the lives of several people on the city's Southside. This home, or what is left of it was a drug house operated by the notorious gang called M.A.F.A.R. MAFIA. As you can see here, an incredible explosion annihilated this home, killing everyone inside. I am told that there were no survivors, but a total of seven people died, and are rumored to be seven of the eight members within the crew that held ranking titles."

Norcotic turned the television off and shook his head slowly.

CHAPTER 6

III

"Go Hard or Go Home"

I t was one in the morning and Shydow pushed his limits working out in his training facility, preparing to crush his next target. His normal routine was intensified. He hadn't turned on his cell phone all day, and for obvious reasons, when you are living the life of a hitman, the less communication you have with any individual, the better. Turning on his cell phone, he saw that there were multiple missed calls that he would return later. There was also a message that came through on his private number that needed immediate attention.

"Enter your password. You have one new message.

First message."

It was a teller at his bank letting him know he had $50,000 deposited into his account from a man named G. Hanging up the phone, Shydow smiled, at the confirmation that his new business associate was serious. Focusing back on his training, Shydow started throwing knives at a target 50 yards away.

"You've got mail."

The announcement from his computer station alerted him that there was an email needing his attention. Shydow stopped his workout and stepped to his computer to check the new email. He recognized the name G attached to a picture of a family. One of the people was circled with the words "KILL HIM" written over them. What really piqued Shydow's interest was the other person in the photo.

It took him by surprise completely, because from the jump the man who called himself G sounded familiar. It wasn't abnormal for his customers to have created a large wealth for themselves. What was interesting is that he had seen this person plenty of times before in person, and in Hip-Hop magazines, and in posters. Shydow now knew who wanted the young boy, Norcotic, dead. It was the owner of G-Fam Records, Rusty.

Norcotic turned his phone on and noticed he had three missed calls from Day-Day. He decided after a long hot shower, and a meal, he would go see Day-Day and tell him that all his friends had died. He knew Day-Day did not care about his partners, but maybe out of respect for him, he would let emotions soar for the dead. Norcotic needed the comfort of his boo, Tra-8, and he knew that if Day-Day would not let him vent, then his girlfriend would. Norcotic was now the last M.A.F.A.R. member alive.

Byrd woke up from a night of passionately fucking Norcotic to see that he had left her apartment. Apparently, he had been gone for a while because the spot where he'd laid was now cold as snow, and she was alone. This reminded her of the time when the only man she ever loved, stole her virginity only for her to wake up and realize she was a "Wham Bam Thank You Girl." Her young mind had her believing his lies and the more Norcotic abused her love and fucked her heart silly, the more she believed they were in love and the more he played her. After becoming so many drug dealers hoe, Byrd finally realized that niggas ain't shit and she started setting niggas up and dating women full time to use them like she'd been used.

Secretly, Byrd had maintained a head over heels kind of love for Norcotic even though she never admitted it or showed it emotionally. She honestly did want him to herself. That's why she envied Tra-8 and vowed to destroy her and Norcotic's relationship no matter what it took. It was only fair that Norcotic introduced the two women with Byrd eventually pretending to be the best friend Tra-8 ever had. With the two women always hanging together, sharing secrets, and going through real shit with each other, they developed a bond and sensual feelings for each other.

Byrd and Tra-8 started to have sex with each other. For Tra-8, it started off as curiosity, then the feelings became surreal. They kept their relationship from Norcotic, and, in their eyes, everything was good with him thinking they were friends. Byrd only had ill intentions from the beginning, as she planned to ruin their relationship and keep Norcotic all to herself. Somehow, she still became jealous when Tra-8 had flirted with that guy at the mall, but she had to play the perfect friend to get her way. She was glad that things happened the way they did because it only added more envious coal to the fire.

After her and Norcotic's long night of pussy and dick

slapping, he was very drained. He was knocked out cold from their sex session. While he lie in her bed, insensible to the world around him, Byrd took pictures and recorded videos of her sucking and slurping on his dick. These are the images that she sent to Tra-8's phone….

After the rape, Tra-8 bought herself a nine- millimeter handgun. She vowed to kill anyone who had the heart to violate her, and she promised to protect herself at all cost. She also wanted to bust a cap in Norcotic's ass for never being on time. She honestly thought he was cheating on her because he was always in the streets with his cell phone turned off. He would literally disappear for days at a time, then say that he was saving money for them to move to Florida. He had gone to Florida one time before, saying that he was planning to move there, only to comeback almost dead by the hands of some Jamaicans. They wanted him dead for dealing with some guy named Pablo Kane. He also had the nerve to be fooling around with some Spanish girl named Enid Adriana R. Feliciano.

Once a cheater, always a cheater. Tra-8 thought to herself more out of hurt and being insecure about cheating on Norcotic more than once; with the last act of infidelity almost ending with her losing her life. She knew that she was not in her right frame of mind, and that she was thinking wrong because her own actions bought these results upon herself. She had put on some black Gucci shades, a black sports bra, and yoga pants with Gucci shoes. Tra-8 was walking to her car getting ready to go to the gun range. Her phone vibrated stopping her in her tracks, and she saw that she had a video message from Byrd. She opened the file, and instantly started to cry fire as if her eyes were the darkest clouds raining turmoil on top of heads burned by brimstone and lava.

Byrd was in the video sucking and slurping on Norcotic's dick passionately. At one point she looked directly into the camera and said, "You a whack ass bitch! And yo man just busted a phat ass nut in this wet ass pussy. So, when he kisses yo dumb ass today, think about how good my booty taste." Tra-8 had seen enough. She called Byrd to confront her about the video and pictures she had sent.

"Hello." Byrd answered the phone like a schoolgirl, trying to sound innocent like she had no idea why Tra-8 was calling her.

"Fuck you, bitch. You ain't shit but a snake ass, project trick. That's how you gon' do me?" Tra-8 yelled.

"I know you ain't talkin Miss holla-at-niggaz-in-my-fucking-face. You was at the mall like we never had a real thing going on."

"Bitch! You the one who told me to holla at the nigga in the first place!" Tra-8 yelled into the phone, continuing to snap. "And for your information the dudes he was with when we got up raped me and robbed Norcotic!"

"Good! You dumb ass bitch! That's what you get. Now maybe you might learn to keep your legs closed!" Byrd laughed through the phone before hanging up in Tra-8's face.

Tra-8 was beyond pissed. She was no longer the good girl that she used to be before being tortured and raped. She planned to let the world know exactly who she was. Now instead of going to the gun range, she planned to stop at Byrd's apartment and use her as a target instead. She continued on to her car. It seemed as luck couldn't have been further away from her at this moment. Norcotic pulled up to the house in a rental car and got out like he never fucked his ex last night.

Norcotic approached Tra-8 who looked like she wanted to kill him and instantly thought that she somehow found out that he fucked Byrd. If looks could kill, Tra-8 would've bodied Norcotic right there, reincarnated him and killed him again. Norcotic wasn't planning on admitting to shit, she would have to prove it, and so he coached himself to just act normal as he approached her. He opened his arms inviting her in for a hug.

"Hey cutie," he said with the most handsome smile he could muster.

Tra-8 saw her chance and slapped that stupid smile right off his face like a human Mr. Potato Head.

SMACK!

"Fuck you do that for!" Norcotic said, holding a hand up to his stinging cheek. It looked like she left a Hamburger Helper glove on the side of his face.

"Because of this!" She yelled at her soon to be ex-boyfriend and held up her phone showing him the pictures and video Byrd sent her.

Norcotic knew there was no reason to keep acting innocent. She had hard evidence and a damn good reason to be acting out of character. Tra-8 started crying again causing eyeliner to escape from behind her shades.

Norcotic just looked on in disbelief as his whole world was coming apart from the core. There was no way things could get any worse, but they did. Tra-8 regained enough composure to take off her shades, wipe her tears, and look Norcotic in his eyes.

"Since everything seems to be coming to light, I have something to tell you. I've been cheating on you too, and guess with who? Byrd!" She spoke in a no nonsense tone.

Norcotic couldn't front, he was hurt, but he expected as

much from Byrd. Even though he knew Byrd would try Tra-8, he thought her loyalty would keep her pure and stable when it came to their relationship.

"Look baby, we've been through a lot together and weathered the storm using our hearts as umbrellas. We both made mistakes, but we can work this shit out, okay?" Norcotic said to her.

Norcotic was trying his best to save his relationship because he loved Tra-8 more than anything in the world. He did not want to lose his baby. It was as if his life was flashing in front of his eyes. He remembered all the good times they had together, with a song he wrote for Tra-8 titled "My Gurl" which played now as a soundtrack to his memories in his mind. When Norcotic wrote the song Tra-8 was in her bed asleep, and as he watched her catch Zzz's , lyrics had just come pouring out of his mind and onto paper.

I went to FL, left you VA/

Where the clouds were grey, hoping for a better day/ I'm talking to my baby Tracie from the BK/

I had something good, now it's gone far away/

I hope and pray that every day I can feel your touch/ And everything will be back to normal, just us/

Looking at the stars bright in the sky/

You had a kiss that made my birthday feel like July/ I wonder why/

I slipped, and had to fuck that bitch/ It made me cry/

I was on some Keith Sweat shit/ I want you back/

But I got to accept my actions/

I fell off when it came to love, guess I was slacking/ But what I was lacking, a nigga now packing/

I'm more into conversation, we can skip the smashing/ It's

plenty of penetration, I don't need no practice/

Yo man so last year, come get with what's happening/

Norcotic snapped out of his daydream with Tra-8 tapping him.

"Norcotic! Norcotic! There's more. Somebody I was dealing with was in the house when I strayed from you, and they stole that combination safe that was in my closet," Tra-8 told him.

"What the fuck you mean somebody stole the safe? Bitch, you better start doing some explaining!" Norcotic snapped, grabbing Tra-8 by the shoulders, shaking her violently.

"Okay!" Tra-8 said, pushing Norcotic off her. "Remember when I went to the mall that day with Byrd?" Tra-8 started.

"Yeah, I remember, Tra-8, Byrd told me you was fucking with some dude there, so what happened? What the fuck that gotta do with my money?" Norcotic asked.

"Well I met someone and…. and." Tra-8 was finding it hard to tell Norcotic what she already told him earlier, because she loved Norcotic but things between them were getting worse and fast and she was starting to cry again. "I cheated on you."

Norcotic couldn't believe what he was hearing. How could he have slipped so far into the streets to the point he was absolutely clueless to what had been going on at home with his woman. Tra-8 already told him she cheated but it was like hearing it for the first time and he was completely dumbfounded.

"So, you just a hoe now? You just gon' let anybody have what I worked on for years to obtain? You a stupid ass bitch, Tra-8. Now there's some nigga out there, you were fucking on the side running around with my money! There was about

$80,000 in that safe. Tra-8, do you know what I had to do to earn that money? I don't know if you're telling the truth, or did you really set me up? I mean how can I trust you?" Tra-8 slapped him again when he finished, and for a while they both just stood there and stared fire into each other's eyes.

It made Tra-8 cry all over again hearing the amount of money that was in that safe. She had no idea there was that much just sitting in her closet because Norcotic was so secretive. He never really told her too much of anything. All she knew was that he was involved in the streets.

"Fuck I look like setting yo dusty ass up, nigga? Even though yo dumbass get on my nerves, I would never betray you like that. Dude drugged my drink. Then he and his homeboys gang raped me. They took everything! Including my innocence, you insensitive prick!" She yelled through tears of pain and she hated herself for crying again.

Norcotic went into a killer's rage and asked why she didn't call him.

"We did call you, Norcotic, but you never answered your phone, you never do! You were probably with that Byrd bitch!" Tra-8 yelled.

Ready to take the life of whoever violated his baby, Norcotic asked Tra-8 who the men were that raped her and stole his money. The answer was one that Norcotic never would have guessed in a million years.

"I was some dude named Ice. He got a tattoo that says "M.A.F.A.R." on his right arm. I didn't think about it at the time, but I think he be with them crazy dudes that be on the news and shit," Tra-8 told him.

Norcotic was crushed! He thought of how everything seemed to be coming together, raising flags of danger and signaling that this was the end. He thought about all the missed call that he never answered, which was probably his girl on the other end crying for help, or just needing his attention. And not getting it, caused her to be unfaithful in the first place. He thought how something so small as a missed call turned his love into hate. He thought about his whole M.A.F.A.R. MAFIA team being dead. He thought about how he would miss Ice's nasty ass sense of humor, but also how his best friend since the second grade raped his woman and stole his money. Norcotic instantly developed a hatred for Ice that he thought he could never have.

Thoughts of Day-Day killing his squad took over his mind, and he remembered all the times Day-Day told him he never liked his crew. He now knew that Day-Day was right. Norcotic did not know exactly how to feel about Day-Day murdering his people. He loved Day-Day like a brother, but he knew M.A.F.A.R. longer. All the thoughts cramming in Norcotic's brain started making his head hurt, and like a conclusion to an unending web of a heart-breaking hypothesis, Norcotic thought about leaving the game and chasing his rap dreams. The realization that his friend had killed his other friends made the young hustler feel it was time to plan for an exit.

In the midst of his thinking, Norcotic never heard Tra-8 talking and calling his name to deliver the most devastating blow in his life. She caught him off guard with an attack that was so treacherous, it nearly caused a heart attack.

"Norcotic, Norcotic, do you hear me?" Tra-8 said, pushing him on his shoulder to get his attention.

"My bad, baby; what you say?"Norcotic asked Tra-8.

"I said, I can't do this no more, we done. Alright?"

Norcotic was at a loss of words like playing Scrabble and only having two letters with no place to play them. His heart felt as if it had fallen off the Titanic as it sunk and splashed in an icy ocean of rejection. Tra- 8 didn't even give Norcotic a chance to give a rebuttal. She just ran, jumped in a car, and left Norcotic lonely in a cloud of dust. Norcotic was formulating a plan to get his girl back as she drove away and left him alone with the pieces of his broken heart. If he knew that would be the last time he'd see Tra-8 alive, he would've fought for her love.

Day-Day watched the whole ordeal from his bedroom window and wondered, *Am I gonna have to kill Norcotic too?* If only he knew Norcotic was marked for death.

CHAPTER 7

III

"Go Hard or Go Home 2"

Rusty was in the kitchen making a tuna salad when he heard arguing in his driveway. He walked over to his sink and quietly opened the window to hear the arguing clearly.

"Norcotic! Norcotic! There's more. Somebody I was dealing with was in the house, and they stole the combination safe that was in my closet."

"What the fuck you mean somebody stole the safe?

Bitch, you better start doing some explaining!"

Rusty had a front row ticket to the Jerry Springer show and as he listened, he could not believe the drama that Norcotic and Tra-8 were going through. The young couple argued back and forth and Rusty loved every second of it because it looked like the couple was on the verge of breaking up. They were fighting hard, and Rusty was getting mad as hell because he could not hear every word like he wanted to.

"Why didn't you call me, Tra-8?"

"We did call you, Norcotic, but you never answered...."

You were probably with that Byrd bitch!" Tra-8 slapped Norcotic a couple of times and Rusty jumped back and grabbed his cheek as if Tra-8 had slapped him.

Norcotic asked Tra-8 who was the person she was cheating on him with, and who stole the safe and her reply even had Rusty shocked.

"It was some dude named Ice. He got a tattoo that says M.A.F.A.R. on his right arm. I didn't think about it at the time, but I think he be with them crazy dudes that be on the news and shit."

Watching the argument play out only enraged Rusty. He knew Norcotic was nothing but trouble, and going against his better judgement, he allowed Tra-8 to date the bum only to have him leading her down the same spiral path as her mother. At that moment, Rusty wished he had not paid Shydow to kill Norcotic because now, he wanted to peel his wig back himself. That gave Rusty a plan to see Norcotic die by his own hands and he acted on it promptly. He called Shydow's phone after seeing Tra-8 and Norcotic go their separate ways and was surprised that he actually answered the phone.

"Hello!" That same evil, robotic voice answered.

"This is G, I have an idea. I don't want you to kill Norcotic anymore," Rusty said only to be cut off by and angry Shydow.

"Noooooo. There is no refunds, a deal is a deal! It's a done deal. Norcotic is marked for death."

Without wasting anymore time, Rusty got down to business.

"Look! I want to kill him myself; I will pay you an extra $400,000 to bring him to me alive."

The phone was silent for a second and then the demon spoke.

"Ok, so be it," Shydow replied.

Rusty smiled an evil grin of revenge hearing Shydow agree with the change of plans. Shydow proceeded.

"When I call you, come to the address that I provide you with. He will be yours today! Wire half of the $400,000 to the same bank account and bring the rest in cash," Shydow said and disconnected the call leaving Rusty head strong about terminating his foe permanently.

Blu was motivated to catch her parents' killer, and delighted that Chauncey, the Director of the FBI, had put her back on the case. She was sure that when he awoke to the puke on his expensive carpet he would've taken her off the case, but he didn't. Within the first 48 hours of the case, Blu had followed some leads and found out that M.A.F.A.R. had something to do with the murders of her parents. Things were getting extremely out of control because all the members of M.A.F.A.R. MAFIA were recently killed in a brutal slaying. There was only one survivor and that was Norcotic, who Rusty said was the main character behind the Governor's Mansion murders. Blu had visited the scene and the whole thing smelled of the work from the hitman Shydow.

A secret manhunt was under way for the man Norcotic, and the one who was rumored to want to kill him, Shydow. The FBI didn't want to alert the men that they were wanted because they would have time to flee the state. But there was a problem in finding Shydow since no one had ever seen his face or even heard his voice. There was no evidence to arrest Norcotic, but enough to question him. Blu stayed up all night digging for information and found out that Norcotic was the son of Block. It was a strange twist of events because Blu's mother, Judge Snuckles-Wilber, had sentenced Block to life in prison under the old law after her father, Governor Douglas Wilber, pardoned him for a killing someone else did. It was too much of a coincidence, so she had to follow the lead.

Blu used her power to gain entrance into the most dangerous prison in America to see Block herself. Before she went into the visitation room, the guards debriefed Blu on the criminal's most recent behavior.

"Lady, it is my duty to inform you that for the past two days, Block had been standing in his cell in the same spot without moving at all!" The guard informed her.

"What?" Blu asked not believing what she had heard.

"The man has not eaten or slept; he is a very dangerous man. Are you sure that you want a visit with this convict?"

"You will be behind very thick bulletproof glass and with armed guards. We have a breach free facility and the best security that the government's money can buy; you will be ok," another guard informed her.

"Yes sir, I would like to see him," Blu responded.

"Good, well when we told him he had a visit he was very happy. He thinks the visit is from his son though. We are not allowed to share visitor information with the prisoners for safety reasons."

Blu was escorted to the visitation room where she waited for Block. Tapping her nails against the metal table rhythmically trying to erase all emotion from her being, Blu was interrupted by Block being escorted into the room. He was a very large man, and she was so glad that the bulletproof glass separated her from the monster. Block walked up to the glass and grabbed the phone off the receiver, so Blu did the same.

"Where's my son?" Are you his bitch or something?" Block asked.

"What! No! I'm…."Blu was ignored and interrupted.

"Where the fuck is my son?" Very big veins the size of teenaged snakes started bulging out of the man's body, and Blu's women's intuition told her something was about to happen, so she tried to gain control of the situation.

"Mister, I'm an FBI agent. My name is Ms…"

BOOM!

Block had cocked back and with lightning speed punched through the bulletproof glass and grabbed Blu by the neck, squeezing so hard that she pissed her pants. All she could think about was the fact that what Block just did was impossible. He had accomplished with his hand what the strongest gun shouldn't be able to do with a bullet. Blu's eyes began to turn red, neglecting her name, and in a matter of time her neck would be broken if she did not get help. The guards on the other side of the glass were beating the man with electric batons, but he just laughed.

One guard aimed a gun at Block's shoulder and fired, it took three shots before Blu was able to escape. She gasped for air while medics and more prison guards rushed to her aid.

"What the fuck was that?" Blu said after finally recuperating.

"That, my lady, was Block." The guard said, pointing in the direction of Block who was now in restraints bleeding from the gunshot wounds. He smiled at her.

"I can smell your pussy from here," he said.

A guard stepped to Block and gave him a lethal blow that knocked the man out cold.

Norcotic sat in his rental car in a deserted area overlooking the lake at Byrd Park in the West end of Richmond. He emptied a Dutch of its guts and inserted a potent mixture of bud that consisted of Purple Haze, Sour Diesel, Kush, and Skunk. Norcotic stuffed the Dutch instead of rolling it up so the blunt was nice and phat. Recalling the past events, Norcotic realized it was time to move on and focus on his career as a rapper. *Maybe it's time to move back to Florida and see what's poppin' with Pablo Kane's nephew, Streets and the Dezel Headbangerz.* Norcotic thought as he puffed on his smoke getting higher by the second. He watched the ducks dip their beaks under the water for the delicious fish that swam underneath.

Relaxed and trapped within his thoughts, Norcotic never noticed the masked man that moved stealthily across the ground like a Navy Seal, creeping up to the car. The human figure of a man in the form of a shadow crossed paths with Norcotic's rear view mirror causing him to ash his blunt and jump to attention. Back on point, he looked around, but saw nothing at all. "Man, I must be trippin'," Norcotic said to himself, lying back in a relaxed position re-lighting his blunt. Soon as he got comfortable, the shadow passed the window again. This time, the shadow was more pronounced, and there was no mistaking that someone was out there.

Norcotic opened his car door and exited the whip with all intentions of whooping somebody's ass. Norcotic was not quick enough as he hopped out of the vehicle, and the shadow figure slapped the butt of a .44 Magnum across Norcotic's nose. As he fell to the ground, the masked man grabbed Norcotic and threw him in the trunk of the rental car speeding off. Norcotic had got caught slipping.

Tra-8 was pulling up in front of Byrd's apartment in Jackson Ward feeling out of place, like an apple in a room full of oranges. Even though she had never killed anyone before, she knew she was going to kill Byrd. Not only did Byrd use her, and cheat on her with her man Norcotic, but she also tricked her into talking to the guy who ended up gang raping her and robbing her boyfriend. Luck was beginning to fall along the line of Tra-8's side or so she thought. Watching Byrd running out of her apartment to meet someone on the corner made Tra-8 feel like she was being given a gift from the gods. To Tra-8's surprise, as she watched Byrd approach her visitor, she realized she knew the man waiting on the corner. It was one of her Uncle Rusty's artists, Dee-I.

What the fuck is going on? Tra-8 thought.

Byrd stood on the corner of Charity and Hickory Street talking to her new boyfriend, Dee-I. She had no idea she was being watched by a female grim reaper. Byrd had met with Dee-I at his video shoot, the same one that Norcotic happened to be attending that led to their night of passion, and the domino effect of chaos.

"What's up?" Dee-I said, licking his lips at Byrd and squeezing her ass as they hugged.

"Nothing Daddy, just waiting on you. I missed you so much, nigga, damn!" Byrd admitted to her new man.

"Did you do what I told you to do, Byrd?" he asked her, pulling away from their embrace.

"Of course, I did what you told me. I'm not that type of bitch, I'm real. I told you that I was going to hold you down."

Dee-I had instructed Byrd to set Norcotic up for him, but

when she told him they used to date he thought she wouldn't do it. All she told him was that knowing Norcotic would make it easier. Dee-I hated that Rusty and Sinister Shan were taking a liking to the new rhyme slayer and he was beyond jealous; he was pissed! If they signed a new artist to G-Fam Records, Dee-I would get secondhand treatment, and he just couldn't have that. He had to put a stop to Norcotic becoming a star even if that meant killing him.

"Good baby," he told Byrd. "If Norcotic ends up breaking Tra-8's heart, Rusty will stop investing in him and that means more money for us."

"I'm with you boy; I told you I got you," Byrd said.

Dee-I looked at her like he was proud of her while thinking to himself, *This bitch just set up her ex for a nigga she just met. What a snake ass bitch*! Dee-I was ready to get away from this thirsty hoe, so he made his move.

"Well look, I gots to go handle some business and shit. The moves I'm about to make will ensure that we stay on top forever."

"Alright Daddy, just get back with me, okay?" Byrd replied.

"I got you, Byrd, so when I come back here, you gon' let me dive in that wet pool pussy?"

"You know you can have me however you want me!" Byrd said, sexually twirling her hips against Dee-I's package.

Dee-I slapped her on the ass and got in his van driving off, leaving the projects in his rear-view mirror.

While Dee-I and Byrd talked, Tra-8 snuck to Byrd's apartment where she found the door left unlocked. She opened the door and crept inside to wait for Byrd to come back to her home. After finding a good hiding spot and pulling out her gun, Tra-8 turned off the lights and readied herself to put a bullet in Byrd's head. Tra-8 never liked the street life so she didn't understand that turning off the lights when she was already in the house, would be the cause of her death.

Byrd made her way back to her apartment skipping like a little girl. She was so happy that she was going to fuck the hottest rapper in Richmond that she didn't care if she looked stupid skipping down the block. Getting closer to her apartment, she noticed the lights were off in her house. *I know I didn't leave the house with the lights off, did I?* She thought to herself while patting her waist to see if the gun she had was still there. Looking around the parking lot for anything suspicious or out of the norm, she spotted something that made her laugh. Tra-8's car was parked in the RRHA building parking lot across the street from her apartment. Byrd could not believe Tra-8 had the balls to come and test her, but Byrd wasn't going to take that shit lightly. She moved towards a plan that would have Tra-8 swimming with the fishes.

CHAPTER 8

"Rest-N-Peace Norcotic"

S hydow stood in an empty warehouse that he bought in a bogus name with his victim tied to a chair. Using a Louisville Slugger bat with a coil of barbed wire around it, Shydow beat the man so bad that he pleaded to die until he couldn't speak due to his teeth choking him. Norcotic could not believe that he had got caught slipping, but with all that was going on in his life, he had let his guard down and now things were about to get real. He wondered if karma would serve him the same fate that all his peers had been served. Shydow picked up his phone, placed a call and waited. When the person answered, Shydow read off an address and hung up. The person he called was G, and Shydow knew that the man was coming to claim the life of Norcotic no matter what. Death was ready to receive another spirit, and hell was definitely waiting for a new occupant.

Rusty was hype. He was glad that he was finally about to get rid of Norcotic. Rusty walked to his Benz with a shotgun and a bag full of money. After punching the address in the GPS, he drove to the destination that Shydow gave him. Rusty thought to himself, *I'm finally ready to get rid of this bitch once and for all.*

Tra-8 crouched low in the dark apartment waiting for Byrd to return so she could hit her with some shells and slump her ass really quick. While Tra-8 waited for her ex-friend to catch some fire, the back door to the apartment opened and Tra-8 didn't waste any time.

BLAOW! BLAOW! BLAOW!

Tra-8 shot three times in the direction of the light coming from the open back door and watched as a body dropped to the floor. She walked over to the slumped figure in case she needed to bust off at close range to finish the job. When she got close enough to the body to see the face, Tra-8 became worried. She did indeed kill somebody, but it wasn't Byrd.

Byrd was very street smart, where Tra-8 was suburban since Byrd was raised her whole like in the ghetto and Tra-8 had been raised by wealthy business owners. Byrd figured Tra-8 was in her house waiting to off her since she saw no signs of her around the projects, and she wasn't going out like that. She devised a quick plan and went to work. Everybody knew Byrd sold drugs, and she decided to use her reputation to her advantage. Byrd walked over to a light skinned crackhead named Ashley and plotted her move.

"Hey Ashley, I need you to do me a favor," Byrd said

trying to sound as if she and Ashley always talked.

Ashley was coming down from a high and was looking for a way to get the monkey off her back.

"I don't do no favors, sweetie." Ashley looked at Byrd with the "Name the Price" face and waited to see if Byrd was going to break bread.

"Alright Ash, damn! I got you. I need you to run up to my apartment, and get my purse off the kitchen table, kay?"

"Since when yo gay ass started carrying a purse?" Ashley said causing Byrd to send a playful jab at Ashley's face to which she ducked with the speed of a seasoned crackhead.

"Mane shut up, and just get the purse. I'll give you $10 and a dub of flav to put on your stem," Byrd offered.

Seeing the opportunity to get high really quick, Ashley took off towards Byrd's apartment to get what she requested.

"Aye Ashley, use the back door cause the front door locked, and don't try to steal none of my shit neither!" Byrd screamed at Ashley's back who never once broke her stride.

After about a minute, Byrd headed to the front door of her apartment and waited…

BLAOW! BLAOW! BLAOW!

When Byrd heard the gunshots, she crept through the front door using the shots to cover the sound of the door closing. Byrd started creeping up the steps with intentions of killing Tra-8.

Tra-8 stood over the dead body in shock. She did not know what to do. She picked up her cell phone and called the police.

"9-1-1. What's your emergency?"

"Yes, a woman has been shot!" Tra-8 informed the operator.

"Okay just stay calm; what's your name and are you in the area of the victim, or…" The operator never got an answer from Tra-8 because as soon as she was about to speak, she heard a familiar voice behind her.

"Die you stank pussy bitch!" Byrd said.

Tra-8 turned around so fast that it startled Byrd shitless. Tra-8 still had her gun in her hand and Byrd was clutching hers, and they both let off multiple shots in each other's directions lighting the apartment like a light show. The apartment now held three dead women, and the police hotline had recorded everything down to the last minute of Byrd and Tra-8's last breaths.

Rusty pulled up to a warehouse along the James River. He looked down at the GPS and made sure he was in the right place and prepared himself to exit the car. It was pitch black outside and from the looks of it, Rusty was in the middle of nowhere. Stepping out of his Benz with the $200,000 in cash in the duffle bag in one hand, and a sawed-off shotgun in his other, Rusty shut his car door and entered the warehouse.

"Shydow! Shydow! Shydow!" Rusty screamed into the darkness only to have his voice echo back to him across the space of time.

His footsteps sounded off loudly, mimicking his pounding heart as he walked inch by inch into the unknown until…

"Nobody has ever seen my face, and I won't start now. Drop the bag of money by your feet and take twenty steps forward." The maniac voice answered back to him.

It was the most intimidating vocalization that ever cursed

the ears, but hearing something familiar while so close to death made Rusty comfortable.

"If you do not follow my instructions, you will be executed along with Norcotic." The voice exclaimed.

Rusty did as he was told and begun nervously walking forward, leaving the payment behind. By the time he got to his tenth step a shadowy figure crossed his path alerting him that something was behind him. Whatever it was moved so fast that Rusty's heart skipped a beat and he frantically turned around and fired a shot in the direction of the money he left behind. When the smoke cleared, Rusty saw nothing, not even the bag of money he had left. That devilish voice was heard again. The wicked laughter was reminiscent of what was heard in scary movies so many times that it became comical, but there was nothing funny about this shit.

"I know you not scared, Rusty. What was you trying to do shooting like that? You almost killed me." The voice said before laughing some more. "Finish what you came to do and get the fuck out of here before I get bored and chop your fucking head off and play basketball with that bitch." Shydow advised his employer who obeyed the command at once.

Rusty did an about face and eyed Norcotic tied to a wooden chair in thick ropes as he took his last ten steps towards his target.

"Good! Now shoot your enemy and then get the fuck out! You have one minute, or you will be executed!" Shydow told Rusty.

"What? Hell no, I'm trying to get close up on this bitch and blow his brains on the fucking floor," Rusty shouted his displeasure. His victim wiggled wildly in the chair as if he were trying to do the Harlem Shake.

He had a black ski mask over his face and his mouth was stuffed and duct taped to keep the scream low, but he still tried to protest his death verbally. Shydow instructed Rusty more.

"No! That's close enough. And for you, time is running out. Handle your business, I got shit to do, G!"

Rusty looked at Norcotic. Even with the ski mask on, you could tell his head was swollen like a pumpkin from being beaten so badly.

"You just couldn't leave her alone, could you? You had to bring your gangsta mentality to my family!" Rusty screamed, squeezing the trigger and emptying the shotgun, sending every shell into Norcotic's body.

The impact of the gauge made Norcotic flip over in the chair. Rusty walked over to his body as it lay on the floor still stuck to the chair. He ignored Shydow's commands to stay away feeling proud of his kill like a lion snagging a zebra. He approached the massacre to see for himself how fucked up Norcotic was because he wanted to remember the vision for the rest of his life.

When Rusty got close and pulled the mask off Norcotic's face, he threw up the tuna salad he had for lunch. He was beaten so badly that he was hard to recognize but it was still painfully obvious that he hadn't killed Norcotic. Rusty instead had shot and killed his son, Day-Day.

As Day-Day listened to Norcotic and Tra-8 argue in the driveway he knew that Norcotic figured out that it was him that had killed his friends of M.A.F.A.R. MAFIA.

Day-Day rationalized that to keep him and his family safe, he would have to kill Norcotic too. When Norcotic left the house Day-Day followed him to Byrd Park, pistol whipped him and put him in the trunk, where he thought he stayed. While Day-Day was at a traffic stop waiting for a green light, the passenger door opened and Norcotic jumped in the seat and put a Glock to Day-Day's head.

"Fuck you, nigga!" Norcotic said, pulling the trigger spilling blood all over the dashboard.

Norcotic muscled Day-Day's body into the backseat and drove to one of his empty properties. When Norcotic pulled up he was shocked to see Day-Day was still alive after a gunshot to the head. He was ready to empty the clip in him but chose to get a bat and hit a couple of homeruns instead. Day-Day was tough, not even the beating after the gunshot killed him, but Norcotic was sure that Rusty would. Even with his brains leaking out of his head, Day-Day wondered, *How in the fuck did Norcotic get out of the trunk of the car and into the passenger seat without me seeing him*? Norcotic laughed thinking to himself about how Day-Day slammed him in the trunk, and when Day-Day went to close it, he stuck a folded up 100-dollar bill in between the locks.

Day-Day shut the trunk thinking it was shut all the way but before Day-Day got in the front seat of the car, Norcotic was out of the trunk and he slammed it at the same time Day-Day closed the driver door. Norcotic rolled under the car and hung on waiting for the perfect time to overcome his victim by moving like a true shadow.

Rusty was extremely pissed.

"Where are you at you son of a bitch!" He screamed on the verge of a nervous breakdown.

Rusty looked around the dark warehouse in search of a live human target to kill, but only saw darkness. Then a taunting laugh filled the warehouse, and Rusty saw a shadow walking towards him. It was not the same evil laugh, which was modified with a voice changer. Shydow had finally grown some balls and Rusty planned to shoot them off. The shadow came closer and started turning from a shadow to a man. The appearance of the man was becoming clearer, and Rusty knew the man was Shydow, but when he saw who he was, he almost shit his pants.

Holding an AR-15 with a devilish grin, Norcotic walked towards Rusty who then aimed his shotgun at him and fired.

CLICK!

Nothing happened. Rusty had used every shell killing his son. Norcotic shook his head mockingly and spoke calmly.

"Every time I saw your face, Rusty, I thought that you looked familiar. Since the last time I saw you, I was too young to remember, I couldn't quite put my finger on it," he started as Rusty listened on feeling defeated. "You used to always come to my mother's house, fucking her while my father rotted in prison."

"What in the hell are you talking about, Norcotic!" Rusty yelled seeing he had nothing to lose and having no clue what Norcotic was talking about.

Shydow kept walking closer, telling a story he knew so well.

"My father was incarcerated for a murder that he never did; my father looked out for you! You did that murder! But my dad never got the money for doing time for a crime he didn't commit, nor did I have a father. I struggled my whole life. Then when he was pardoned, he was set up again! And you go blame my lifestyle on being unworthy to fuck with Tra-8. Nigga fuck you!

It now dawned on Rusty that Shydow, aka Norcotic, was the son of Block. Rusty had killed a man back in the 80s and never did the time for it because the Brown's Brother Gang set up a man named Block to take the charge. Clayton Brown was working with one of Rusty's family members and they devised a plan to get someone else to fall for the murder that Rusty committed. Now, talking to Block's son in the flesh, he wished he had never done what he did.

"Yeah, I didn't think it was you until I got my hands on the pictures from Governor Wilber's house," Norcotic continued.

"Wait a minute!" Rusty interrupted. "What do you mean Governor Wilber's house? It was you who pulled off the murders at the Mansion?" he asked Shydow, who never responded.

Rusty had told Blu that it was Norcotic but that was just to set Norcotic up. He never thought it was actually true. It seemed now history was coming back to bite him in more ways than one.

Norcotic threw the pictures at Rusty's feet. When Rusty picked them up and looked at them, he now understood that Norcotic knew more than what he thought he did. One of the pictures was Governor Douglas Wilber buying large amounts of cocaine from Clayton Brown with Rusty standing right next to the governor. Rusty looked up from the pictures at the AR-15 pointed directly at him. Norcotic looked right into Rusty's eyes.

"Motherfucking Rusty Wilber, you're the governor's brother," he said before emptying the whole clip into Rusty's body.

Every bullet hit its target and tore Rusty's stomach open, leaking his organs all over the floor. Norcotic sat down on the floor and thought of all the crazy shit that had transpired. His girlfriend's uncle was Governor Douglas Wilber's brother, and he had killed him viciously. Then it hit him. Day-Day knew about the robbery, so why didn't he try to stop him? He now knew there was more to Day-Day's not wanting to go on the heist. He dug his mind and recalled a conversation they had on the matter of robbing the Mansion.

"Yo Norcotic, if robbing that spot will help you get your father home, do your thing. I never really had my father in my life, and when he was around, we won't cool like that. Don't get this big house and money confused; it's just a shell to cover the truth," Day-Day said.

"That's some real shit, Day-Day, but you know we need you for this heist, bruh!"

"Naw son, I'm good. I don't rock with yo M.A.F.A.R. niggas like that. It's just something about them niggas, real talk. Just make it out in one piece."

Norcotic sat and cried tears of turmoil as he picked up his untraceable phone and called the police. He used his voice changer and gave the dispatcher the address to the warehouse where father and son lie dead together.

"This is Channel 12 News with breaking coverage this morning. Richmond City has seen one of its bloodiest weeks in history as a string of murders seem to be all connected to one another. Governor Douglas Wilber was found, body burned and battered along with his wife, Judge Snuckles-Wilber inside of the Governor's Mansion. They died with a group of Richmond City Police Officers who responded to the Mansion being targeted by gunmen who were never captured and are still at large. The couple was responsible for releasing a man who was not guilty of a murder on a pardon named Block. Block killed a drug kingpin upon his release, by the name of Clayton Brown and Judge Snuckles-Wilber sentenced him to life in prison. The governor's brother, the CEO of G-Fam Records, Rusty Wilber, was found murdered next to his son, Day-Day, with shocking photos and a recorded videotape of the Wilber brothers buying cocaine in large quantities from none other than Clayton Brown. Rusty's niece, Tra-8 was also found shot to death this morning in the Jackson Ward project apartment complex in what seems like a love triangle gone wrong. It was also discovered that two .357 Magnums with Day-Day's fingerprints were linked to the murders of a group of men known as M.A.F.A.R. MAFIA. This is truly a sad day, and...."

Block turned off the television in his cell and relaxed for the first time in years.

Norcotic was sitting on a plane that was designated to land in Orlando, Florida. Norcotic cried tears of turmoil 30,000 feet in the air because that was the closest he was going to get to heaven to let Tra-8 know that he loved her and that he was so sorry for the pain he caused her. There was a kid sitting next to him on the plane bobbing his head to some music through his headphones on his iPod. The kid and another, whom Norcotic assumed was his brother, began to fight over who would listen to the music next.

"Give me the damn music!" a woman who could have

only been the boys' mother said, reaching for the iPod.

When she grabbed the iPod, it fell and Norcotic got up out of his seat to help the woman retrieve it. Norcotic picked it up and curiosity took over him. Norcotic wanted to know what musician the boys had been so hype over, so after looking at the iPod he gave it back to the owners. Norcotic saw the words across the screen and thought it was some kind of weird joke.

Sinister Shan presents: NORCOTIC: "It's Coming Freestyle" single.

Norcotic looked at the two boys who were looking back as if wondering if the bigger boy was going to give them their iPod back. Norcotic asked the boys who the artist was, and where they got the song from while handing the iPod to the boys' mother.

"Are you stupid or something, mister? That's Norcotic on Sinister Shan's mixtape; the song is everywhere." The boys gave each other a high five while their mother told them to mind their manners.

Norcotic looked at their mother and offered his hand in a greeting.

"Forgive my own manners, lady, my name is Nor, and you are?"

The woman looked at Norcotic for a second and then shook his hand.

"Hi, my name is Blu."

Bringing his attention back to the boys, he asked if he could listen to the song.

"Sure," the boys said at the same time like spiritual twins.

Their mom handed him the iPod.

Listening to the song, Norcotic realized that this was the freestyle that he did in the G-Fam studio when he first met

Sinister Shan. Norcotic had no idea that Shan would put the song on his mixtape. Norcotic bobbed his head to the music thinking, *Sinister Shan is a monster! He's hands down the best DJ in the world!* Lost in a world of music, Norcotic never noticed that Dee-I was on the same plane watching him with a look of murder in his eyes.

TO BE CONTINUED....

ABOUT THE AUTHOR

Russell (Norcotic) Mabry is a Hip-Hop artist, actor, and author born and raised in Richmond, VA. Norcotic overcame the streets which claimed the lives of many of his associates with the two things that motivated him towards a life outside of the ghetto, MusikNMoney. As the son of Richmond VA's Legend Block, he travels the world with the goal of becoming the greatest writer ever.

 IG: @Norcotic804

 FB: Laray Mabry

Listen to music from Norcotic on:

 IHeartRadio
https://www.iheart.com/artist/norcotic-34765276/

 YouTube
https://www.youtube.com/channel/UCx51MN2jeK1Xb OXMAIXJkZw

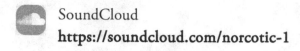

SoundCloud
https://soundcloud.com/norcotic-1

DatPiff
https://www.datpiff.com/Norcotic-Go-hard-or-go-home-mixtape.3491.html

ABOUT THE BOOK

A story about revenge and jealousy. A young man looking to avenge his father finds an outlet in music. Among him is an array of potential friends and enemies looking to stop him. With a life of crime resulting from the acts of revenge and jealousy among his team, how will he survive? Will he succeed?

CPSIA information can be obtained
at www.ICGtesting.com
Printed in the USA
LVHW090808281220
675096LV00013B/477